THE SCOTTISH CAT

THE SCOTTISH CAT

edited by
Hamish Whyte

ABERDEEN UNIVERSITY PRESS

First published in 1987
Aberdeen University Press
A member of the Pergamon Group

© Hamish Whyte 1987

British Library Cataloguing in Publication Data

The Scottish cat: an anthology.
  1. English literature—Scottish authors
  2. Cats in literature
  I. Whyte, Hamish
  820.8'036   PR8636.5.C3

  ISBN 0 08 035077 1
  ISBN 0 08 035078 X (Pbk)

Typeset by Pindar (Scotland) Limited, Edinburgh

PRINTED IN GREAT BRITAIN BY
THE UNIVERSITY PRESS
ABERDEEN

CONTENTS

CONTENTS

MAGICAL CATS

PROVERBIAL CATS

WILDCATS

CAT AND MOUSE

LITERARY CATS

POETICAL CATS

CAT TALES

This book is for Kenneth and Christina
and in memory of
Inky, Oedipus, Sappho, Pippin and Saki

CAT

Mine be the house where you would find
A woman in her right mind,
A cat to walk among the books,
And friends about at any time —
I bear no fruit without these roots.

GUILLAUME APOLLINAIRE, transl by EDWIN MORGAN

ACKNOWLEDGEMENTS

I should like to thank the many friends, colleagues and interested parties who have contributed to *The Scottish Cat* either by encouragement or by suggesting items for inclusion: Tom Berry, Moira Burgess, Ian Campbell, Dr James C Corson, Deirdre Craig, Hazel Daiches, Anne Escott, Tom Fenton, Joe Fisher, Sheila Forrest, Anne and Peter Harrison, Jolyon Hudson, Elspeth King, Kevin McCarra, Carl MacDougall, Anne McPherson, Oscar Marzaroli, Edwin Morgan, Alyson Niven, George Oliver, Roy O'Neil, Jenny Rutt, Enda Ryan and Nick Whistler.

Particular thanks go to Simon Berry for his enthusiasm and support for the 'Pussy Baudrons' book and for his knack of finding out-of-the-way snippets of information; and to cat-mad Barbara Robertson for her superb drawings, made especially for the book.

The stock of The Mitchell Library, Glasgow, was a major resource; thanks there to Moira Thorburn for photographing many of the illustrations.

I am most grateful to the copyright owners and contributors who allowed work to be included (see pp. 203 to 209 for the complete list of contributors and sources).

Thanks also to Colin MacLean and Marjorie Leith of AUP for their interest and care. And to Winifred, thanks for her unfailing aid behind the lines without which this book (and all the rest) could not have been completed.

INTRODUCTION

The Scottish Cat began as a chauvinistic exercise. The French are regarded as the literary cat lovers *par excellence*, but the question occurred: could the other partner in the Auld Alliance show a similar interest in cats? The only examples of cats associated with Scotland that came to mind were the wildcat and Sir Walter Scott's pet, Hinse — and wasn't Compton Mackenzie supposed to have been cat-daft? However, starting with Christabel Aberconway's admirable *A Dictionary of Cat Lovers*, a wealth of material began to reveal itself; friends joined the hunt and came up with some unusual stories from unlikely sources, and serendipity played its usual part. The literature ranged from the fifteenth century to the present; and a link with France was established by the discovery that the first book solely devoted to cats, *Lettres sur les Chats* (1727), was written by the son of a Scots emigré to Paris, Francois de Moncrif.

A goodly number of cat lovers appeared — Scott, Joanna Baillie, Carlyle, Andrew Lang, Willa Muir, Compton Mackenzie, Sydney Goodsir Smith — but the high proportion of ailurophobes was surprising. Generally speaking, the Scots seem to have treated cats pretty shamefully — as scapegoats, objects of sport or instruments of magic, for example, as witness the roasting of cats alive in the ghastly ceremony of the Taigheirm, the cruel pastime of cat in the barrel and the baptising and drowning of a cat by the North Berwick witches. Whether any or all of these events actually happened is beside the point — the attitude towards cats (and other animals too) is unmistakable. And towards the wildcat there was a determined policy of extermination. This has lessened in recent years but now there are fears that the wildcat may be extinct as a 'pure race' owing to widespread inter-breeding with domestic animals (see *The Scotsman* 3, 6 and 13 March 1987). The Nature Conservancy Council is currently working on a research programme into the genetics of the wildcat: indications are that there are still pure wildcats around (as well as wild cats), but the controversy will no doubt continue.

Incidentally, the wildcat, as well as providing an example of fierce independence for Scots, has by its agility added to the language in the phrase, *tummle one's wilkies* (tumble head over heels). The following quotation gives the derivation: 'I would have actually turned a somersault,

Jake. Andrew Burke (1980)

or, as the expression in Scotland is, "tummel'd the wul'-cat".' (George Mills, *The Beggar's Benison*, 1866)

The Englishman Thomas Pennant describing Highland customs on his tour of 1769 noted: 'All fire is extinguished where a corps is kept; and it is reckoned so ominous, for a dog or cat to pass over it, that the poor animal is killed without mercy.' Neil Munro records that as a boy he received a present of a catapult with a note attached: 'From an uncle who does not like cats.' (Perhaps he was confused as to the origin of the word catapult.) And Maurice Lindsay in his poem 'Certain Killers' expresses that feeling of unease that many people, including even some ailurophiles, have in the presence of cats.

However, the record is not all bad. Cats which have always been tolerated if not loved are those valued for their usefulness — the working cats, like the famous Glenturret Distillery mouser, a female tortoiseshell called Towser (born in 1963 on the Queen's birthday, 21 April and died 20 March 1987), now enshrined in *The Guinness Book of Records* as having dispatched over 27,000 mice, averaging three per day. Glasgow's current favourite is Smudge, a black and white 12 lb female who works at the People's Palace on Glasgow Green and who is a fully paid-up member of the GMBATU; she also has the distinction of having been reproduced in china, by the Scottish artist Margery Clinton — and sold as 'replicats'. The Glasgow Sheriff Court cat Misty made a small headline in 1968 when she was accidentally driven away while sleeping on top of the axle of a car parked outside the court. After a police alert she was eventually tracked down near Balloch and returned to Glasgow where she was reported to be back in the custody of the Court, 'on a diet of fish and milk'.

According to legend the Scots were the first northern people to keep cats: Fergus I of Scotland (fl. 330 BC) is said to have brought them from Portugal, his ancestors having taken cats there from Egypt. Whatever the case, there have been cats, wild and domestic, in Scotland for a long time. *The Scottish Cat* offers a representative selection from the range of material: nursery rhymes, fairy tales, poems of praise, elegies, stories of love and terror — from Henryson's Aesopian fable of the town and country mice, through seventeenth century witchcraft, nineteenth century literary life and letters, to Edwin Morgan's clever contemporary concrete cats, with illustrations from a wide variety of sources, published and unpublished. Regrettably, not everything could be included. Some cats, such as Aileen Paterson's Maisie and George Mackay Brown's Fankle can be found in most good bookshops; others are not so easily come by. A list of further reading is provided for those wishing to continue the pleasant pursuit of the Scottish cat.

CRADLE CATS

In the Nursery Rhymes, the cat always has precedence
COMPTON MACKENZIE, *Cats' Company*

The cat is one of the oldest domestic pets, so it is not surprising to find it featured prominently in nursery rhymes. In fact, there are at least a dozen traditional Scottish cat rhymes and many more literary ones. 'Pussy-cat, Pussy-cat' is probably the best known of all nursery rhymes; the Scottish version ('Poussie, poussie baudrons') first appeared in print in the 1842 edition of Chambers's *The Popular Rhymes of Scotland*, with the cat going to see the *king* and the 'guid fat mousikie' merely a 'wee mousie': the version printed here is from the 1870 edition. Baudrons, by the way, is the familiar Scots name for cat.

Two children's poems whose authors are known are included: a modern 'bairnsang' by J K Annand, from one of his three collections of children's verse, and one in Shetlandic by Peter Jamieson.

TRADITIONAL NURSERY RHYMES

Poussie, poussie, baudrons,
Where hae ye been?
I've been at London
To see the queen!

Poussie, poussie, baudrons,
What got ye there?
I got a guid fat mousikie
Rinnin' up a stair!

Poussie, poussie, baudrons,
What did ye do wi't?
I put it in my meal-pock,
To eat it to my bread!

There was a wee bit mousikie,
That lived in Gilberaty, O;
It couldna get a bite o cheese,
For cheetie-pussie-cattie, O.

I said unto the cheesikie,
'O fain would I be at you, O,
If it werena for the cruel paws
Of cheetie-pussie-cattie, O'.

Madam Pussie's coming hame,
Riding on a grey stane.
What's tae the supper?
Pease brose and butter.

Who'll say the grace?
I'll say the grace.
Leviticus, Levaticus,
Taste, taste, taste!

Jean, Jean, Jean
The cat's at the cream,
Supping with her forefeet,
And glowering with her een.

The cattie rade to Paisley, to Paisley, to Paisley,
The cattie rade to Paisley upon a harrow tine;
And she came louping hame again,
And she came louping hame again,
And she came louping hame again
Upon a mare o mine.
It was upon a Wednesday,
A windy, windy Wednesday,
It was upon a Wednesday,
Gin I can rightly mind.

Sing, sing!
What shall I sing?
The cat ran awa
With my apron string.

Mousie, mousie, come to me,
The cat's awa frae hame,
Mousie, mousie, come to me,
I'll use you kind and make you tame.

Lingle, lingle, lang tang,
Our cat's deid!
What did she die with?
With a sair heid!

All you that kent her,
When she was alive,
Come tae her burial,
Atween four and five.

The grey cat's kittled in Charlie's wig,
The grey cat's kittled in Charlie's wig;
There's one of them living and two of them dead,
The grey cat's kittled in Charlie's wig.

Pussie at the fireside
   Suppin' up brose,
Doon came a cinder
   And burnt pussy's nose
Och, said pussy,
   That's no fair.
Weel, said the cinder,
   Ye shouldna been there.

THE CAT

Creeping by night
Creeping by night
Creeping by night
  said the grey cat.

Creeping by night
With neither star nor gleam
Nor brightness, nor light
  said the grey cat.

   Trans from the Gaelic
by IAIN CRICHTON SMITH

CAT AND MOUS

Said the poussie
Til the mousie,
'Let me intil
Your wee housie.
We will play
And we will sing
And we will dance
A jingo-ring.'

Said the mousie
Til the poussie,
'Ye'll no get
In my wee housie.
Ye are big
And I am wee
And ye wad eat me
For your tea.'

J K ANNAND

DA CAT AN DA MOOSE
(*A Bairn Sang*)

Da cat sat be da fire,
  Neebin, neebin;
Da moose kam oot a holl,
  Lunkin, lunkin.

'Whaar's du gyaain, du pooshin,
  Skulkin, skulkin?'
'Never du anse whaar I'm gyaain,
  Purranin, purranin!'

'Feth, I'll fell dee,
  Limmer, limmer!'
'Nenn o dee nemm-kaa'n,
  Spyaaler, spyaaler!'

'Limme win at dee,
  Murti, murti!'
'Whit'll du doe,
  Voaleri, voaleri?'

'I'll sort dee, I'll sort dee,
  Peesterin, peesterin!'
'Yah, sae weel du will,
  Venderin, venderin!'

'Oh, limme win oot-be,
  Skrovveler, skrovveler!'
'Come dee wis, dan,
  Whisker, whisker!'

'Here I spang noo,
  Waa-cattle, waa-cattle!'
'I can spang toe,
  Essi-pattle, essi-pattle!'

'Wait 'ee dan, wait 'ee dan,
  Broona, broona!'
'Weel, I hae nae hurry,
  Kloora, kloora!'

'I sanna lat dee preev,
  Foiti, foiti!'
'We'll see aboot dat,
  Nyirmi, nyirmi!'

'Wha fell i da kirn,
  Klooksi, klooksi?'
'Bit I wan oot ageng,
  Vengi, vengi!'

'I'll gyit dee diss time,
    Skunneri, skunneri!'
'Yah, meybe du will,
    Krami, krami!'

Da cat gae a seich
    An fell ower neebin;
Da moose gae a gaf
    An begood preevin.

PETER JAMIESON

Copper fittings to a hall door. Talwin Morris (1897)

CATS' COMPANY

Cats as companions can be useful, as they were to Alexander Selkirk on his island, or they can be familiars, as they were to the author of 'The Bookseller's Cat', being at once 'decorative — contemplative — philosophical', though not everybody would agree with him that 'a wife cannot compare except to her disadvantage.' A cat can be a companion for all seasons and all conditions, as Joanna Baillie's poem, 'The Kitten', illustrates. What it means to be parted from a beloved cat is described in the poem James Thomson, author of 'The Seasons', wrote for his sister Elizabeth. And the death of a working cat (in a weaving factory) is lamented by Ellen Johnston in Dundee in the 1860s. The story of the loss of the painter Sam Bough's cat Bung might sum up the feelings of all who have suffered a similar loss of a pet: for months after, Bough would follow every black cat he saw, calling out, 'Bung! Bung! poor Bung!'

BAUDRON'S SANG

The gudewife birrs wi the wheel a day,
Three threeds an a thrum,
Three threeds an a thrum,
A walth o wark an sma time for play,
Wi the lint sae white an worset grey,
Work hard she maun, while sing I may —
Three threeds an a thrum,
Three threeds an a thrum.

The gudewife rises out o her bed,
Three threeds an a thrum,
Three threeds an a thrum,
Wi her cozy nicht-mutch around her head,
To steer the fire to a blaze sae red,
Her feet I rub wi welcome glad,
Three threeds an a thrum,
Three threeds an a thrum.

I dander round her wi blythsome birr,
Three threeds an a thrum,
Three threeds an a thrum,
An rub on her legs my sleek warm fur,
Wi sweeps o my tail I welcome her,
An round her rin wherever she stir,
Three threeds an a thrum,
Three threeds an a thrum.

The men folks' time for rest is gie sma —
Three threeds an a thrum,
Three threeds an a thrum,
They're out in sunshine, an out in snaw;
Tho cauld winds whistle, or rain should fa,
I, i the ingle, do nought ava;
Three threeds an a thrum,
Three threeds an a thrum.

I like the gudeman, but loe the wife,
Three threeds an a thrum,
Three threeds an a thrum,
Days mony they've seen o toil, an strife,
O sorrow the human hours are rife,
Their hands been mine a the days o my life,
Three threeds an a thrum,
Three threeds an a thrum.

Auld baudrons grey, she kittened me here,
Three threeds an a thrum,
Three threeds an a thrum,
An wha was my sire, I ne'er did speir;
Brithers an sisters smoored i the weir,
Left me alane to my mither dear,
Three threeds an a thrum,
Three threeds an a thrum.

An syne she loed me muckle mair,
Three threeds an a thrum,
Three threeds an a thrum,
For want o her weans near a taen frae'r
Her only kitten she couldna spare,
I a healing was to her heart sae sair,
Three threeds an a thrum,
Three threeds an a thrum.

As I grew a cat, wi look sae douce,
Three threeds an a thrum,
Three threeds an a thrum,
She learnt me to catch the pilfrin moose,
Wi the thief-like rottens I had nae truce,
But banished them frae the maister's hoose,
Three threeds an a thrum,
Three threeds an a thrum.

Mither got fushionless, auld an blin,
Three threeds an a thrum,
Three threeds an a thrum,

The bluid in her veins was cauld an thin,
Her claws were blunt an she couldna rin,
An tae her forebears she was gathered in,
Three threeds an a thrum,
Three threeds an a thrum.

Now I sit hurklin aye i the ase,
Three threeds an a thrum,
Three threeds an a thrum,
The queen I am o that cosy place;
As wi ilka paw I dicht my face,
I sing an purr wi mickle grace,
Three threeds an a thrum,
Three threeds an a thrum.

John Anderson my Jo. Engraving by David Allan from Robert Burns *Works*
(1834–36)

CRUSOE'S CATS

Alexander Selkirk, who was rendered famous by Mons. de Foe, under the name of Robinson Crusoe, was born in Largo, 1676. His history, divested of fable, is as follows:

Having gone to sea in his youth, and in the year 1703, being sailing master of the ship 'Cinque Ports', Captain Stradling, bound for the South Seas, he was put on shore on the island of Juan Fernandez, as a punishment for mutiny. In that solitude he remained for four years and four months, from which he was at last relieved and brought to England by Captain Woods Rogers. He had with him in the island his clothes and bedding, with a firelock, some powder, bullets and tobacco, a hatchet, knife, kettle, his mathematical instruments, and Bible. He built two huts of Pimento trees, and covered them with long grass, and in a short time lined them with skins of goats which he killed with his musket, so long as his powder lasted (which at first was but a pound); when that was spent he caught them by speed of foot. Having learned to produce fire by rubbing two pieces of wood together, he dressed his victuals in one of his huts and slept in the other, which was at some distance from his kitchen. A multitude of rats often disturbed his repose by gnawing his feet and other parts of his body, which induced him to feed a number of cats for his protection. In a short time these became so tame that they would lie about him in hundreds, and soon delivered him from the rats, his enemies. Upon his return, he declared to his friends that nothing gave him so much uneasiness as the thoughts, that when he died his body would be devoured by those very cats he had with so much care tamed and fed. To divert his mind from such melancholy thoughts, he would sometimes dance and sing among his kids and goats, at other times retire to his devotion.

from The Parish of Largo by the Rev Mr Spence Oliphant, in *The Statistical Account of Scotland* vol IV, 1792, pp 544–5

The following two anecdotes are taken from *Traditions of Edinburgh* by Robert Chambers (1802–71) the Edinburgh publisher and editor of *The Popular Rhymes of Scotland*. The first concerns Lord Coalstoun, a judge who in 1757 lived on the fourth floor of a tenement in the Luckenbooths, and his unexpected encounter with a kitten; the other describes the kindness to cats of Christian, the daughter of the poet Allan Ramsay (1685–1758).

LORD COALSTOUN AND HIS WIG

A strange accident one morning befell Lord Coalstoun while residing in this house. It was at that time the custom for advocates, and no less for judges, to dress themselves in gown, wig, and cravat at their own houses, and to walk in a sort of state, thus rigged out, with their cocked hats in their hands, to the Parliament House. They usually breakfasted early, and when dressed would occasionally lean over their parlour windows, for a few minutes before St Giles's bell sounded the starting peal of a quarter to nine, enjoying the morning air, such as it was, and perhaps discussing the news of the day, or the convivialities of the preceding evening, with a neighbouring advocate on the opposite side of the alley. It so happened that one morning, while Lord Coalstoun was preparing to enjoy his matutinal treat, two girls, who lived in the second floor above, were amusing themselves with a kitten, which, in thoughtless sport, they had swung over the window by a cord tied round its middle, and hoisted for some time up and down, till the creature was getting rather desperate with its exertions. In this crisis his lordship popped his head out of the window directly below that from which the kitten swung, little suspecting, good easy man, what a danger impended, like the sword of Damocles, over his head, hung, too, by a single — not *hair*, 'tis true, but scarcely more responsible material — *garter*, when down came the exasperated animal at full career directly upon his senatorial wig. No sooner did the girls perceive what sort of a landing-place their kitten had found than, in terror and surprise, they began to draw it up; but this measure was now too late, for along with the animal up also came the judge's wig, fixed full in its determined talons. His lordship's surprise on finding his wig lifted off his head was much increased when, on looking up, he perceived it dangling its way upwards, without any means visible to him by which its motions might be accounted for. The astonishment, the dread, the almost *awe* of the senator below — the half mirth, half terror of the girls above — together with the fierce and relentless energy of retention on the part of Puss between — altogether formed a scene to which language could not easily do justice. It was a joke soon explained and pardoned; but assuredly the perpetrators of it did afterwards get many lengthened injunctions from their parents never again to fish over the window, with such a bait, for honest men's wigs.

CHRISTIAN RAMSAY'S CATS

[Allan Ramsay's] daughter Christian, an amiable, kind-hearted woman, said to possess a gift of verse, lived for many years in New Street. At seventy-four she had the misfortune to be thrown down by a hackney-coach, and had her leg broken; yet she recovered, and lived to the age of eighty-eight. Leading a solitary life, she took a great fancy for cats. Besides supporting many in her own house, curiously disposed in bandboxes, with doors to go in and out at, she caused food to be laid out for others on her stair and around her house. Not a word of obloquy would she listen to against the species, alleging, when any wickedness of a cat was spoken of, that the animal must have acted under provocation, for by nature, she asserted, cats are harmless. Often did her maid go with morning messages to her friends, inquiring, with her compliments, after their pet cats.

LISY'S PARTING WITH HER CAT

The dreadful hour with leaden pace approached,
Lashed fiercely on by unrelenting fate,
When Lisy and her bosom Cat must part:
For now, to school and pensive needle doomed,
She's banished from her childhood's undashed joy,
And all the pleasing intercourse she kept
With her grey comrade, which has often soothed
Her tender moments while the world around
Glowed with ambition, business, and vice,
Or lay dissolved in sleep's delicious arms;
And from their dewy orbs the conscious stars
Shed on their friendship influence benign.
    But see where mournful Puss, advancing, stood
With outstretched tail, casts looks of anxious woe
On melting Lisy, in whose eyes the tear
Stood tremulous, and thus would fain have said,
If Nature had not tied her struggling tongue:
'Unkind, O! who shall now with fattening milk,
With flesh, with bread, and fish beloved, and meat,
Regale my taste? and at the cheerful fire,
Ah, who shall bask me in their downy lap?
Who shall invite me to the bed, and throw
The bedclothes o'er me in the winter night,
When Eurus roars? Beneath whose soothing hand
Soft shall I purr? But now, when Lisy's gone,
What is the dull officious world to me?
I loathe the thoughts of life.' Thus plained the cat,
While Lisy felt, by sympathetic touch,
These anxious thoughts that in her mind revolved,
And casting on her a desponding look,
She snatched her in her arms with eager grief,
And mewing, thus began: 'O Cat beloved!
Thou dear companion of my tender years!
Joy of my youth! that oft has licked my hands
With velvet tongue ne'er stained by mouse's blood.
Oh, gentle Cat! how shall I part with thee?
How dead and heavy will the moments pass

When you are not in my delighted eye,
With Cubi playing, or your flying tail.
How harshly will the softest muslin feel,
And all the silk of schools, while I no more
Have your sleek skin to soothe my softened sense?
How shall I eat while you are not beside
To share the bit? How shall I ever sleep
While I no more your lulling murmurs hear?
Yet we must part — so rigid fate decrees —
But never shall your loved idea dear
Part from my soul, and when I first can mark
The embroidered figure on the snowy lawn,
Your image shall my needle keen employ.
Hark! now I'm called away! O direful sound!
I come — I come, but first I charge you all —
You — you — and you, particularly you,
O, Mary, Mary, feed her with the best,
Repose her nightly in the warmest couch,
And be a Lisy to her!' — Having said,
She set her down, and with her head across,
Rushed to the evil which she could not shun,
While a sad mew went knelling to her heart!

JAMES THOMSON (1700–48)

THE KITTEN

Wanton droll, whose harmless play
Beguiles the rustic's closing day,
When, drawn the evening fire about,
Sit aged crone and thoughtless lout,
And child upon his three-foot stool,
Waiting until his supper cool,
And maid, whose cheek outblooms the rose,
As bright the blazing fagot glows,
Who, bending to the friendly light,
Plies her task with busy sleight;
Come, show thy tricks and sportive graces,
Thus circled round with merry faces!

Backward coil'd and crouching low,
With glaring eyeballs watch thy foe,
The housewife's spindle whirling round,
Or thread or straw that on the ground
Its shadow throws, by urchin sly
Held out to lure thy roving eye;
Then stealing onward, fiercely spring
Upon the tempting faithless thing.
Now, wheeling round with bootless skill,
Thy bo-peep tail provokes thee still,
As still beyond thy curving side
Its jetty tip is seen to glide;
Till from thy centre starting far,
Thou sidelong veerst with rump in air
Erected stiff, and gait awry,
Like madam in her tantrums high;
Though ne'er a madam of them all,
Whose silken kirtle sweeps the hall,
More varied trick and whim displays
To catch the admiring stranger's gaze.

Doth power in measured verses dwell,
All thy vagaries wild to tell?
Ah no! the start, the jet, the bound,
The giddy scamper round and round,
With leap and toss and high curvet,
And many a whirling somerset,
(Permitted by the modern muse
Expression technical to use)
These mock the deftest rhymester's skill,
But poor in art, though rich in will.

The featest tumbler, stage bedight,
To thee is but a clumsy wight,
Who every limb and sinew strains
To do what costs thee little pains;
For which, I trow, the gaping crowd
Requite him oft with plaudits loud.

But, stopp'd the while thy wanton play,
Applauses too thy pains repay:
For then, beneath some urchin's hand
With modest pride thou tak'st thy stand,
While many a stroke of kindness glides
Along thy back and tabby sides.
Dilated swells thy glossy fur,
And loudly croons thy busy purr,
As, timing well the equal sound,
Thy clutching feet bepat the ground,
And all their harmless claws disclose
Like prickles of an early rose,
While softly from thy whisker'd cheek
Thy half-closed eyes peer, mild and meek.

But not alone by cottage fire
Do rustics rude thy feats admire.
The learned sage, whose thoughts explore
The widest range of human lore,
Or with unfetter'd fancy fly
Through airy heights of poesy,
Pausing smiles with alter'd air
To see thee climb his elbow-chair,
Or, struggling on the mat below,
Hold warfare with his slipper'd toe.

Aquatint by David Allan from Allan Ramsay *The Gentle Shepherd* (1786)

The widow'd dame or lonely maid,
Who, in the still but cheerless shade
Of home unsocial, spends her age,
And rarely turns a letter'd page,
Upon her hearth for thee lets fall
The rounded cork or paper ball,
Nor chides thee on thy wicked watch,
The ends of ravell'd skein to catch,
But lets thee have thy wayward will,
Perplexing oft her better skill.

E'en he, whose mind of gloomy bent,
In lonely tower or prison pent,
Reviews the coil of former days,
And loathes the world and all its ways.
What time the lamp's unsteady gleam
Hath roused him from his moody dream,
Feels, as thou gambol'st round his seat,
His heart of pride less fiercely beat,
And smiles, a link in thee to find,
That joins it still to living kind.

Whence hast thou then, thou witless puss!
The magic power to charm us thus?
Is it that in thy glaring eye
And rapid movements, we descry —
Whilst we at ease, secure from ill,
The chimney corner snugly fill —
A lion darting on his prey,
A tiger at his ruthless play?
Or is it that in thee we trace,
With all thy varied wanton grace,
An emblem, view'd with kindred eye,
Of tricky, restless infancy?
Ah! many a lightly sportive child,
Who hath like thee our wits beguiled,
To dull and sober manhood grown,
With strange recoil our hearts disown.

And so, poor kit! must thou endure,
When thou becom'st a cat demure,
Full many a cuff and angry word,
Chased roughly from the tempting board.

But yet, for that thou hast, I ween,
So oft our favour'd play-mate been,
Soft be the change which thou shalt prove!
When time hath spoil'd thee of our love,
Still be thou deem'd by housewife fat
A comely, careful, mousing cat,
Whose dish is, for the public good,
Replenish'd oft with savoury food,
Nor, when thy span of life is past,
Be thou to pond or dung-hill cast,
But, gently borne on goodman's spade,
Beneath the decent sod be laid;
And children show with glistening eyes
The place where poor old pussy lies.

JOANNA BAILLIE (1762–1851)

Stable Trouble. James Howe

MOTION FOR PROTECTING CATS

This letter to the Editor appeared under the above heading in the Glasgow periodical *The Literary Reporter*, 25 October 1823. Spoof or not it obviously reflected some feeling current at the time.

A number of ladies, on this side the water, have formed themselves into a select party, or society, for the express purpose of enquiring into the state of the civic economy of the lower orders of beings, especially including the feline and minor-canine species, and how far the social treatment of these beings is compatible with justice, and reciprocal comfort. I have taken the liberty, (as correspondents say; but I assure you, Sir, I would not take liberties) of submitting to you for insertion, a few remarks I have made on the general treatment of that much injured race of beings — Cats.

It may be a foible of mine, but I never mention the name of that noble animal, without engendering that prejudice for silver-toned words and phrases, which *Cat*egorically distinguish the writings of an enthusiast. But, Oh, how few there are alive to such sensations! — *Cat*alani, I am told, is possessed of a kindred feeling; and never have I experienced moments of greater delight — never has my flexible spirit been bowed down to more sympathetic affection, than when the dulcet falsetto of *Cat*alani, has approached the virgin tone of my delightful Tom. Cats are partial to sweet savours; and sweet Mr Southey has thus described it as proceeding from a portion of feeling nearly intellectual, when, on describing a Cat, wandering among, and rubbing herself against the fairest flowers, he says, 'she courts the odours of the hand that formed the flowers.' You will excuse me, Mr Editor, if in this essay, I rub myself against a few flowers of speech, in respect to the animal, of which we see so much, and yet know so little.

I had an idea of giving you my sentiments on the above subject, with the purpose of *Cat*echising the persecutors of that meritorious animal; when by giving a *Cat*alogue of some of the enormities, it has been my lot to witness from my residence, I trusted that should I have not been enabled to reach the *ears* of the laws of this country, I might have been enabled to reach the *hearts* of my feeling country-women. Oh, that I had the power to give a *Cat*apultan overthrow to those monsters in the shape of men, who have proclaimed that a Cat has *nine* lives! — It is thus that the rising generation, whom I have witnessed, make so light of taking the life of a Cat, on the ground that she has plenty more to spare. Tell it not in christendom, that we have laws, which make capital the transgression of sheep-stealing — which make felonious the act of dog-stealing — of pigeon-luring — hare-snaring and pig-stealing, and is there one institute for preserving even the life of a Cat? — Spirit of Whittington be still! — Oh, ye biped murderers! how long will ye continue to lave your hands in the blood of that faithful attendant, who has spent her life in your service, and in keeping watch over your basket and your store.

It has been for some time, but more generally since the election of the *new* police commissioners, the practice of a number of vagrant boys to assemble with their dogs each afternoon on the banks of the river, when some furry victim was unbagged in the water, and a hunt was commenced by the vagrants and their vile dogs at the life of an innocent Cat. How often have I been roused to an indignation beyond my sex, on witnessing the worse than *Cat*aline conspiracy against the lives of these innocents, practised in the most horrid barbarities before my eyes. It was but this afternoon I sent Jenny down with sixpence to save the life of a most decent-looking pussy; but, after the villains had received the price of her ransom, their dogs tore the cat from her arms. If these cruelties are to be practised with impunity, Sir, have we not a reason to suspect that these atrocities may extend to beings of a higher order? And with these matters before our eyes, it is that our philanthropic society, have determined to lay aside all furry apparel whatsoever; being well assured that the various sorts of muffs, tippets, and furs, are furnished by a process practised much nearer home than Russia. You will agree with me, Sir, that our suspicions were far from being unconfirmed by the appearance of a hawker, at some of our doors, enquiring for hare or *Cat* skins, which he offered to purchase. I could scarcely credit my senses, as I beheld him eye my dear Tommy with a speculation that seemed founded on experience. My blood curdled within me at the sight of the horrid wretch. I felt myself on the point of relaxing into a *Cat*arrh; I raved on dear Mr S——y, our old police commissioner, to apprehend the murderer; when the villain left me saying, he believed I was 'an old Tabby,' and he would like no better than skin me himself! I am sorry for trespassing on the bounds of this sheet; but the head and tail of my writing is, that you must *Cat*er some remedy for our distresses as early as possible.

SARAH SINGLE
Hutchisontown, 20 October, 1823

THE OLD TOM CAT
Air: The Ivy Green

A downy cove is our old tom cat,
    Just turned thirty years old;
He eateth the lean, and leaveth the fat,
    And won't touch his meals when too cold.
His food must be crumbled, and not decay'd,
    To pleasure his dainty whim,
But a turkey bone from the kitchen-maid,
    Is a very good meal for him.

Chorus: Creeping over the tiles pit pat,
        A downy cove is the old tom cat.

Whole joints have fled, and their bones decayed,
    And dishes have broken been,
But old tom still follows the kitchen-maid,
    And slyly licks up the cream.

Pantry. *Northern Looking Glass* (1825)

Now, old tom cat, in his lonely days,
   Shall joyously think of the past,
And a big leg of mutton, that never was touched,
   Shall be food for our Tommy at last.

Chorus

Fast creepeth he, though he hath no wings,
   And a sly old dodger is he,
As under the garret window he sings —
   Ain't you coming out tonight, love, to me?
Then slyly he creepeth the gutters all round,
   And his old tail he joyously waves,
As his lady love from a garret he spies,
   And he sings her his amorous staves.

Chorus

(This song was sung by 'the renowned' PADDY
MCGOWN in the Shakspere Saloon, Glasgow, in
1855. It was printed at the Poet's Box, 6 St
Andrew's Lane, and sold as a penny broadsheet.)

TWO SKYE CATS

The Rev Norman Macleod (1812–72), editor of *Good Words*, received this
tale of feline sabbath-breaking in a letter from a Skye man about 1866.

Dear Sir
   I am going to tell you a small skitch about two cats I had in my time
one of them was a thief and a Sabath Breaker the other was Honest and
kept the Sabath in 1845 i think I left Glasgow for Skye where I belong
to my father had a small farm I was nine years there every one kent
about the Botatoe failure there in one of these years my father parted
this lif in 23 May My mother on 12th August my wife 1st Jany same
year leaving me with five young children the oldest between ten and
eleven years old the youngest a smart Boy this day never saw a mother
yet I sent the child to nurs at 15s a month I kept with them for two
years fighting between death and life at last on the brink of starving I

told them at last that I would have to leave them that if possible I would send som suport from Glasge I got eight shillings for som straw I had I left them one shilly and 7 to pay the boat they waited for the steamboat on Saterday until late but no relief on Saterday night they went home and slept till late on Sunday when they got up they were without a morsel of meat a sure of rain came on the old las went out and told her sister to go with her and gather some small botatoes that was coming in sight where the botatoes was planted they took home a small Pot full and put them on the fire I had two splendid cats mother and daughter as whit as snow except a few black spots on the tail and on the head they were both Standing to the fire one of the children said if we had some kitchen now with that small Pot of botatoes we would be all right but in a short time one of the cats came in with a fish laid that beside the fire before he halted he tok in a fish to each of them but when he was at the dor with the fifth fish the holy cat that stood at the fire all the time would have the last to himself I think it should be given to the publick but you are the best Judge.

DONALD MACLEOD, *Memoir of Norman Macleod*, 1876

The Cotter's Saturday Night. Engraving by David Allan from Robert Burns *Works* (1834–36)

CALLANDER, FIFE AND EDINBURGH CATS

'One day . . . it struck me that I should like to try and write a book about Cats. I mentioned the idea to some of my friends: the first burst out laughing . . . The second said there were a hundred books about Cats already. The third said, "Nobody would read it."' So wrote the Victorian humorist Charles Henry Ross in *The Book of Cats* (1868). It is probably not much read nowadays, which is a pity for it is an amusing compendium of, as the subtitle says, 'Feline Facts and Fancies, Legendary, Lyrical, Medical, Mirthful and Miscellaneous.' These three short extracts demonstrate some of the remarkable powers cats have.

A family in Callander had in their possession a favourite Tom Cat, which had, upon several occasions, exhibited more than ordinary sagacity. One day, Tom made off with a piece of beef, and the servant followed him cautiously, with the intention of catching, and administering to him a little wholesome correction. To her amazement, she saw the Cat go to a corner of the yard where she knew a rat-hole existed, and lay the beef down by the side of it. Leaving the beef there, he hid himself a short distance off, and watched until a rat made its appearance. Tom's tail then began to wag, and just as the rat was moving away with the bait, he sprang upon, and killed it.

In 1819 a favourite Tabby belonging to a shipmaster was left on shore, by accident, while his vessel sailed from the harbour of Aberdour, Fifeshire, which is about half a mile from the village. The vessel was a month absent, and on her return, to the astonishment of the shipmaster, Puss came on board with a fine stout kitten in her mouth, apparently about three weeks old, and went directly down into the cabin. Two others of her young ones were afterwards caught, quite wild, in a neighbouring wood, where she must have remained with them until the return of the ship. The shipmaster did not allow her, again, to go on shore, otherwise it is probable she would have brought all her family on board. It was very remarkable, because vessels were daily going in and out of the harbour, none of which she ever thought of visiting till the one she had left returned.

Maisie goes to Glasgow. Aileen Paterson

A lady residing in Glasgow had a handsome Cat sent to her from Edinburgh: it was conveyed to her in a close basket in a carriage. The animal was carefully watched for two months; but having produced a pair of young ones at the end of that time, she was left to her own discretion, which she very soon employed in disappearing with both her kittens. The lady at Glasgow wrote to her friend at Edinburgh, deploring her loss, and the Cat was supposed to have formed some new attachment. About a fortnight, however, after her disappearance from Glasgow, her well-known mew was heard at the street-door of her Edinburgh mistress; and there she was with both her kittens, they in the best state, but she, herself, very thin. It is clear that she could carry only one kitten at a time. The distance from Glasgow to Edinburgh is forty-four miles, so that if she brought one kitten part of the way, and then went back for the other, and thus conveyed them alternately, she must have travelled 120 miles at least. She, also, must have journeyed only during the night, and must have resorted to many other precautions for the safety of her young.

SAM BOUGH'S CAT BUNG

Sam Bough (1822–78), the Scottish landscape painter, though born in Carlisle, lived the second half of his life in Edinburgh, settling there in 1855 having been a scene painter in Manchester and Glasgow. The following extract is taken from Sidney Gilpin's account of his life.

At one time or another, Bough was partial to Newfoundlands, Skye terriers, Dandie Dinmonts, Italian greyhounds, and other breeds of dogs. He was also very fond of cats. A big black one especially — bought by his sister Ann for a penny from some boys in Glasgow — was much petted at table, and had the run of the house. This cat suddenly disappeared, and its loss was mourned many days. A handsome reward was offered for its recovery, and for months after the event, Bough could not resist running after every sable-coated tabby he saw, calling out in a coaxing way, 'Bung! Bung! poor Bung!'

There was still another 'Bung', of a later generation, and the last of its name. This cat lived to a great age — something like seventeen years. When getting old and grey, it became subject to frequent fits of sulky peevishness, and used sometimes to poke its claws from under the table unceremoniously into 'Sacchi's' [the bull-dog's] face, and, at other times, into its blind eye. Through a long course of luxurious living, this cat became very choice in its dietary, and, being fed mostly on cream, remained very fat and sleek of coat till the day of its death.

SIDNEY GILPIN, *Sam Bough, RSA* (1905)

NELLY'S LAMENT FOR THE PIRNHOUSE CAT
KILLED BY THE ELEVATOR, C——E FACTORY, DUNDEE

Oh! fare-ye-weel my bonnie cat,
Nae mair I'll smooth yer skin sae black.
Mony a time I stroked yer back,
      Puir wee creator;
Ye've gane yer last lang sleep tae tak'.
      The Elevator

Has sent ye aff tae your lang hame,
Whaur hunger ne'er will jag yer wame,
Whaur ye shall ne'er put in a claim
      For meal or milk;
Yer in the 'pond,' free frae a' blame,
      Boiled like a whelk.

Puir hapless beast, what was't that took
Ye hunting into yon dark nook?
Whaur 'Death' sat cooring wi' his hook
      Tae nip yer neck.
I'll think upon yer deein' look
      Wi' sad respect.

My very brain ran roon about
When I saw Archie tak' ye oot,
Wi' scalped pow and bluidy snoot.
      Heigh, when I think,
A stane tied roon yer neck, nae doot
      Tae gar ye sink.

Jist yesterday, my bonnie beast,
I held ye close unto my breast;
When, ye as proud as ony priest,
      Did cock yer lug;
Syne aff ye ran tae get a feast
      Frae yer milk mug.

But noo nae mair in oor pirnhouse
Ye'll hunt the rats, nor catch a moose,
Nor on the counter sit fu' douse,
      And mew and yell,
And shoot yer humph sae prude and spruce
      At rhyming Nell.

Your race upon the earth was ran,
Puir puss, ere it was weel began;
Ye've gane whaur beastie, boy, and man
      Are doomed tae go.
Omnipotence in His vast plan
      Ordained it so.

There's nane has deign'd tae mourn ye here,
Unless mysel' wi' grief sincere;
Though but a cat I'll still revere
      Thy worth wi' pity.
And ower yer memory drap a tear,
      Puir wee cheetie.

ELLEN JOHNSTON, 'The Factory Girl' (d. 1873)

The Glenturret Distillery Cat, Towser

THE BOOKSELLER'S CAT

I have written that I am all alone in my shop but, these last months, I have had a cat for company.

A cat is the ideal literary companion. A wife, I am sure, cannot compare except to her disadvantage. A dog is out of the question. It may do at a butcher's — it would be out of place in a bookseller's. A cat for a bookseller is a different creature temperamentally from the same animal at a fishmonger's or a baker's. In these shops the cat is a useful animal — I suppose it is employed to eat fish entrails or to keep down rats and mice — but in my shop its function is that of a familiar. It is at once decorative — contemplative — philosophical, and it begets in me great calm and contentment.

My cat has discrimination. On Sundays — it will hardly be believed — she lies on a large old-fashioned Family Bible. This Bible I bought most uncommercially from a woman who had had it bequeathed to her. She was no scoffer at sacred things or one of those who undervalue the Holy Writ. Her lot was different. She was the survivor of a pious family and had heired the Family Bible of her parents through her eldest brother and in turn four other Bibles — no less ponderous than the one I bought from her — through the successive deaths of her two brothers and two sisters. With such a cargo of Holy Books and a further blessing of many children she sought to lighten her load of both by commerce with me. She heard — Heaven knows what gossip — about my pliable and simple character from the greengrocer and it was armed with an introduction from her that she sought me. I bought the heavy tome. It measures a foot by a foot and a half and is — from a bookseller's view — a real book. No bookshelf would hold it. It is made to lie — I imagine — if no lectern had been made for it, on some lace-edged cloth of bygone days on top of some high and stately chest of drawers.

This Bible is described on the title page as 'The Practical and Devotional Family Bible' and is of Scottish origin. The date is in Roman figures — 1858 — and it was 'printed by William Collins & Co and sold by William Collins, South Hanover Street, Glasgow.' It contains the Old and New Testaments 'according to the Authorised Version, with the Marginal Readings, and original and selected parallel references, printed at length, and the Commentaries of Henry and Scott, condensed by the Rev John McFarlane, LLD, Glasgow.'

That is a digression, but I went to my front shop and brought the Book that I might write down its proper description. This Bible lies on top of a fixture of smaller shelves nearest to my west window and it catches the sun. This fact — and the softness of its leather binding — may have led the cat to choose it for a resting place — I don't know — but anyway on many a Sunday — entering my shop in the afternoon to see that all was right (really because I can't leave the blessed place a whole day unvisited) I find my cat curled up on top of this noble book.

I am not claiming that my cat is a pious cat, however, though I am perhaps as serious a devotee of its species as the ordinary Egyptians were reputed to be. I admire the cat for its independence. It has no slavish faithfulness like a dog. It does not fawn. The nearest approach to a manifestation of affection that my cat attains is to rub itself against my legs when I come in with my purchase of liver. I love its languorous grace then — like the seductive, alluring wiles of some wondrously beautiful, entirely selfish woman that I can imagine, but will never know.

I can believe that cats were in Egypt considered sacred animals. I read that they were held to be under the special protection of PASHT — a great goddess — and that again, they were held to be servants of Diana. They behave to-day certainly as if they owe no allegiance to mortal master or mistress, but either have already pledged their souls away or hold them aloof from all earthly entanglements.

I have few books on cats, I find. The reference books tell how hated cats were in the Middle Ages and how their association with old women who were believed to be witches brought many to horrible deaths. Indeed it was part of some mediaeval processions to imprison a number of cats in a wicker cage and slowly roast the squalling crate of misery over a brazier as the masque went through the streets. Well may my cat with these race memories find peace in our time reclining on the Sacred Book!

There is an excellent book which I got once specially for a customer on the cat. It is by Carl Van Vechten and is called the *Tiger in the House*. It is an American book and I kept it long enough to see that it was a very elaborate compilation of all that was known, imagined and written about cats. The pictures — some of them anyway — were good, but I have no longer the book by me.

Cats have always been favourites with remarkable men — (I bow to myself) from Richelieu — who had many of them always by him — to Dr Nikola — to me quite as real a character — on whose shoulder a cat always sat. I trained mine to do that at meal times and it is an entertainment to watch her reach out her paw and detain my hand — fork-laden — on its way to my mouth. I rarely can resist a reminder so gentle.

I like my cat in all the aspects of her mystically obscure personality, but now — at this time — she is almost terrible. She is in the throes of passion — and all my efforts are required to keep her from escaping from the shop on some adventurous amour. I play the stern parent and deny her what she hardly knows she is seeking. I seek to compel her contentment — as mine is compelled — by the bookshop we live in, but hers is a straining nature — determined — daring — ready to risk all — and I fear that somehow she will elude me — defeat me — and win her heart's desire on the house-tops.

WILLIAM Y DARLING (1885–1962),
The Private Papers of a Bankrupt Bookseller, 1931

CONNOISSEURS

Under a tree I read a Latin book,
And there, in seeming slumber, lies my cat;
Each of us thinking, with our harmless look,
Of this and that.

Such singing — prettier than any words —
O singers you are sweet and well-to-do!
My cat, who has the finest taste in birds,
Thinks so too.

DUGALD S MACCOLL (1859–1948)

I COMFORT MY CAT

The Great Beast in the sky,
more terrifying to my cat than aeroplanes,
growls and she runs to me for comfort.

I know that the Beast is a thunderstorm
but my cat does not know it.
I can feel the thunder currents vibrating through my nerves;
my cat feels them too through hers.
I can transmit comfort with voice and hands.

Knowing, feeling, giving comfort,
in one fused moment
I am altogether human.
Unknowing, feeling, accepting comfort,
my cat is wholly cat.

WILLA MUIR (1890–1970),
Laconics, jingles and other verses, 1969

BOWZER

For a number of years there was a great tiger cat that lived in the byre. He was a magnificent brute and could poach a rabbit as well as any dog. When we brought him home he often jumped in the room window with a full-grown rabbit in his mouth.

At the time he was in the byres, however, he was quite unapproachable to any one but myself. I don't know how we became friends but I used to lie and play with him for hours on end. Whenever any one came on the scene he would be off like a streak of tawny lightning. For his size and bulk his speed was amazing.

Bowzer wasn't always in the byre at night: his habits were nomadic and irregular. But if he were anywhere about he always came and clawed at my stockings. Sometimes he would follow me back to the house when a word from my father would send him streaking off into the night.

We had a magnificent Persian cat at home. Beauty was her name. She was an aristocratic but gentle dame and never had any kittens. I hadn't the same affection for her as I had for Bowzer. But then Beauty never paid much attention to me and disliked being pawed. She must have eaten poison about the woods for she came home sick one morning and died.

Her successor, of the same breed and pedigree, was a splendid Tom called Jellicoe. He was an intelligent and friendly beast, easily trained to do a variety of tricks. One summer afternoon, when he was dozing on a dyke close by the house, the gamekeeper came along and emptied a couple of barrels into him.

It was shortly after this that Bowzer was brought down from the byre. We found he despised milk, liked his tea strong with plenty of sugar and had an inordinate passion for cheese. His sweet tooth soon led him to master the technique of opening 8 lb biscuit tins. For a time it was thought that I was the guilty party. But Bowzer's intelligence did not take him the length of replacing the lid and he was ultimately found out. After this he got his ration of biscuits with the rest of the family.

Bowzer earned his keep: he was not tolerated for purely sentimental reasons. Keeping hens in the garden encouraged rats. But Bowzer made short work of them for he was an excellent ratter. My mother had no great opinion of dogs. Once, when working on a Galloway farm, she had bought a dog whose qualities as a ratter had been loudly praised. But the rats came and chased him away from his dinner with the result that she had to stand guard over his dish in order to prevent him dying of starvation. It appears that this kindness was not altogether lost on the brute for he became an excellent cattle dog. Finally he became so courageous that he bit an infant sister as she lay in the cradle — whereupon he was unceremoniously dragged out and shot.

When we knew we were leaving Tulliallan, Bowzer was handed over to the village grocer who was also plagued with rats and who had tried several breeds of dogs without success. Inside a week Bowzer had liquidated the rats. But it was not till about a month later that the grocer discovered he had eaten his way into the heart of a hundredweight cheese (from the side screened by the wall) and consumed a very considerable poundage of his finest sweet biscuits.

The last time I was in the grocer's shop Bowzer was basking resplendently on the counter and there seemed to have settled on his countenance the most beatific feline beam I have ever seen. He was fat and sleek and prosperous and completely at his ease. The gay ribbon with which the grocer's pretty daughter had adorned his neck added the final touch indicative of his complete bourgeoisification. But he came and gnawed at my finger in the most friendly fashion, licked my face and purred like a super-charged racing car. I remembered the days when we had played together on the granary floor and gone to sleep together in the hay: and since he showed no desire to follow me out of the shop I returned home disconsolate. When he died it was probably from fatty degeneration of the heart.

JAMES BARKE (1905–1958),
The Green Hills Far Away (1940)

DID THE CAT *KNOW*?

Smudge, a marmalade she-cat, with a white chest and paws, was desperately ill. The vet didn't hold out much hope of her living. But he did what he could for her. We left her in a hay-filled box with high sides, in a corner of the kitchen. As a favour to me, it seemed, rather than to please herself, she consented to lick a few drops of cream off the tip of my finger. She wouldn't touch either food or milk.

Then, when one would have doubted her ability to get out of the box, let alone walk across the room, she disappeared, and was nowhere to be found.

During the days we were looking for her I frequently caught sight of a tom cat slinking around the farm, and doing a disappearing act whenever anyone appeared. I knew him well by sight. He was semi-wild, and was often to be seen hunting in the wood, Dubh Charin. He was the father of more than one of Smudge's litters of kittens.

'Smudge has had it,' I said, 'I don't think she stands a chance on her own.'

The days passed, then one morning Smudge walked into the kitchen, looking well. She arched her back and began to purr.

We were all delighted, but mystified, too, as to how she had managed to survive. Anyway, she took up residence in the kitchen again, and we left the window open to allow her to come and go as she pleased. Whilst forking down hay a day or so later in the old farmhouse, I came across the nest she had made for herself, right on top, in which to convalesce. If there was any doubt about this having

been HER nest, bits of recently killed mouse, and the like, in the immediate area put the matter beyond any such doubts. But how had she managed to hunt for herself?

From now on we found, each morning, a trail of muddy pawmarks over the white enamelled surface of the washing machine by the kitchen window, showing how a cat had come and gone, presumably Smudge. And each morning we found a fresh offering on the kitchen floor — a mole, a vole, a mouse, and once, a young rat.

I have a writing-room, a cubby-hole of a place off the kitchen passage. It is warm, and, as well as a desk, has an armchair. One night, without thinking, I closed the door on Smudge whilst she slept in the chair. Next morning we found the usual pad marks across the surface of the washing machine, and yet another mole in the middle of the floor.

'Where is Smudge?' my wife asked. I suddenly remembered shutting her in my room, and went to look. She was still there, asleep. I automatically looked towards the window, to see if it was shut and, just as I did so, caught a glimpse of the tom cat jumping from the window sill and making off along a garden path. The window was shut.

The explanation now seemed obvious. When Smudge was sick she had crawled away, to make herself a nest on top of the hay. The tom cat had hunted for her and fed her. He had gone on trying to feed her long after she was capable of fending for herself.

This little episode left us with two unanswered questions. How had Smudge known from the start that the tom cat would look after her? Why had he bothered in any case?

We will never know for certain, but the whole thing was made more interesting when we discovered that Smudge was to have kittens, which must have been conceived before she fell ill, and, undoubtedly, the tom cat was their father.

CAMPBELL K FINLAY

MAGICAL CATS

Cats make occasional appearances in Scottish folk lore, but most frequently in accounts of Scottish witchcraft and witch trials; either as instruments of magic — usually sacrificed for a specific end — or as one of the animals that witches were apparently able to change themselves into — hares and mice being other favourites: spells are recorded for this, such as the one given by Isobel Gowdie in 1662. In Scotland for some reason cats (or other animals) never featured as domestic familiars of witches in the sense they did in England: spirits or imps in the shape of small animals kept and fed by a witch and used for working magic on persons and property.

Cats are often associated with the weather, particularly at sea, in folk tradition, as forecasters. For instance, if a cat washes behind her ears it will rain ('True Calendars, as Pusses eare/ Washt o're, to tell what change is neare.' — Herrick); if a cat is frolicsome there may be a storm coming; she can raise the wind by whipping the water with her paw, or even scratching a chair or table leg. It was a logical development of this sort of tradition — from forecasting to actually causing — that witches should use cats as a means of raising storms or causing death, as the North Berwick witches attempted in 1590.

An early note of scepticism about such beliefs in the supernatural abilities of cats was sounded in 1702 by Robert Wodrow (1679–1734), minister of Eastwood, Renfrewshire. A correspondent, Mr Jameson, had written: 'Its told me and pretended by sensible persons to be very true that no male cats live in Kaitness, and yet the femells bring forth store of young, being impregnated only by eating at some time of the year some 5 corns of barlie stipped or sodden in sweet milk.' Wodrow replied: 'I thank you for your physicall observation anent the catts of Caithness. I have not soe much philosophicall faith as to believe your informer to have been deuly searched in this case. I shall be glad to have Doctor Sibbalds opinion on it.' (For Dr Sibbald see section on Wild Cats)

WITCHES AND CATS

From the evidence of the Scottish witch trials the cat would appear to have been a common sacrificial animal, often baptized before being killed. At Lang Niddry in 1608 witches performed a rite in which they christened a cat 'and callit hir Margaret: And thaireftir come all bak agane to . . . qhair first thai convenit, and cuist the kat to the Devill.' (Pitcairn II, 542) In 1630 an Alexander Hamilton was alleged to have had converse with the Devil near Edinburgh who appeared in the guise of either a cat, crow, or dog. Hamilton claimed to cure one Thomas Home of his sickness:

> for this effect the said Alexr schortlie thereftir past to clarkingtoun burne besyde the rottoneraw haifing ane katt under his okister [oxter-armpit] and thair wt his said battoun raisit Sathan his maister quha than appeirit to him in the liknes of ane corbie and thair instructit him be quhat meanis he sould cure the said Thomas of his said seiknes and he haifing ressauit that respons fra the devill the said Alexr thereftir cuist to him the kat quha vanischet away. (Quoted by Margaret Murray in *The Witch-Cult in Western Europe*, 1962 edition, p 208)

In 1590 members of a coven of witches at North Berwick confessed to an attempt to drown King James VI by raising a storm to wreck the ship carrying him and his bride from Denmark. A cat was the means to this end. The leader of these witches, John Fian, was

> Fylit, for the chaissing of ane catt in Tranent; in the quhilk chaise, he was careit heich aboue the ground, with gryt swyftnes, and as lychtlie as the catt hir selff, ower ane heicher dyke, nor he was able to lay his hand to the heid off: And being inquyrit, to quhat effect he chaissit the samin? Ansuerit, that in ane conventioune haldin at Brumhoillis, Sathan commandit all that wer present, to tak cattis; lyke as, he, for obedience to Sathan, chaisit the said catt, purpoislie to be cassin in the sea, to raise windis for distructioune of schippis and boittis. (Pitcairn II, ii, 212)

Agnes Sampson of the same coven confessed

> . . . that at the time when his Majestie was in Denmarke, shee being accompanied by the parties before speciallie named, tooke a cat and

christened it, and afterward bounde to each part of that cat, the cheefest parte of a dead man, and severall joyntis of his bodie: And that in the night following, the saide cat was convayed into the middest of the sea by all these witches, sayling in their riddles or cives, as is aforesaid, and so left the saide cat right before the towne of Lieth in Scotland. This doone, there did arise such a tempest in the sea, as a greater hath not bene seene; which tempest was the cause of the perishing of a boat or vessell comming over from the towne of Brunt Ilande to the towne of Lieth, wherein was sundrie jewelles and rich giftes, which should have beene presented to the now Queene of Scotland, at her Majesties coming to Leith. Againe, it is confessed, that the saide christened cat was the cause that the Kinges Majesties shippe, at his comming forth of Denmarke, had a contrarie winde to the rest of his shippes then being in his companie; which thing was most strange and true, as the Kinges Majestie acknowledgeth, for when the rest of the shippes had a faire and good winde, then was the winde contrarie and altogether against his Majestie; and further, the sayde witche declared, that his Majestie had never come safely from the sea, if his faith had not prevayled above their intentions.

This sensationalised account is taken from a newssheet, *Newes from Scotland*, 1591 (Pitcairn I, ii, 218); the legal record gives a more sober, and more detailed, version of the 'christening':

Agnes Sampsoune, Jonett Campbell, Johnne Fean, Gelie Duncan and Meg Dyn baptesit ane catt in the wobstaris hous, in maner following: Fyrst, twa of thame held ane fingar, in the ane syd of the chimnay cruik, and ane vther held ane vther fingar in the vther syd, the twa nebbis of the fingaris meting togidder; than thay patt the catt thryis throw the linkis of the cruik, and passit itt thryis vnder the chimnay. Thaireftir, att Begie Toddis hous, thay knitt to the foure feit of the catt, foure jountis of men; quhilk being done, the sayd Jonet fechit it to Leith; and about mydnycht, sche and the twa Linkhop, and twa wyfeis callit Stobbeis, came to the Peir-heid, and saying thir wordis, 'See that thair be na defait amangis ws;' and thay caist the catt in the see, sa far as thay mycht, quhilk swam owre and cam agane; and thay that wer in the Panis, caist in ane vthir catt in the see att xj houris. Eftir quhilk, be thair insorcerie and inchantment, the boit perischit betuix Leith and Kinghorne: quhilk thing the Dewill did, and went before, with ane stalf in his hand. (Pitcairn I, ii, 237)

THE TAIGHEIRM

This 'conjuring of cats' was peculiar to Scotland; it is not recorded elsewhere. Margaret Murray thinks it is derived from an early form of sacrifice. There could hardly be a more barbarous sacrifice of cats than the Taigheirm.

The Taigheirm was an infernal magical sacrifice of cats, the origin of which lies in the remotest pagan times, and in rites dedicated to the subterranean gods, from whom men solicited, by nocturnal offerings, particular gifts and benefits. Through Christianity these sacrifices were modified; and instead of being made to the subterranean powers, they were now made to the infernal ones; or, as they were called in the Highlands and Western Isles of Scotland, the Black-Cat Spirits. Whence these sacrifices came to the Western Isles is not known, but most probably it was from the farthest north, as the Western Isles were peopled from Iceland, Norway, and the Faroe Isles, and were dependent on and connected with those countries till the later Christian ages.

According to Horst's Deuteroscopy, black cats were indispensable to the incantation ceremony of the Taigheirm, and these were dedicated to the subterranean gods, or, later, to the demons of Christianity. The midnight hour, between Friday and Saturday, was the authentic time for these horrible practices and invocations; and the sacrifice was continued four whole days and nights, without the operator taking any nourishment. 'After the cats were dedicated to all the devils, and put into a magico-sympathetic condition by the shameful things done to them, and the agony occasioned them, one of them was at once put upon the spit, and, amid terrific howlings, roasted before a slow fire. The moment that the howls of one tortured cat ceased in death, another was put upon the spit, for a minute of interval must not take place if they would control hell; and this continued for the four entire days and nights. If the exorcist could hold it out still longer, and even till his physical powers were absolutely exhausted, he must do so.'

After a certain continuance of the sacrifice, infernal spirits appeared in the shape of black cats. There came continually more and more of these cats; and their howlings, mingled with those of the cats roasting on the spit, were terrific. Finally appeared a cat of a monstrous size,

Aquatint by David Allan from Allan Ramsay *The Gentle Shepherd* (1786)

with dreadful menaces. When the Taigheirm was complete, the sacrificer demanded of the spirits the reward of his offering, which consisted of various things; as riches, children, food, and clothing. The gift of second-sight, which they had not had before, was, however, the usual recompense; and they retained it to the day of their death. The connection of these ceremonies with those of the Schamans of Northern Asia, and of the witch practices of the middle ages, is obvious.

The offering of cats is remarkable, for it was also practised by the ancient Egyptians. Not only in Scotland, but throughout all Europe, cats were sacrificed to the subterranean gods, as a peculiarly effective means of coming into communication with the powers of darkness.

One of the last Taigheirm, according to Horst, was held in the middle of the seventeenth century on the island of Mull. The inhabitants still show the place where Allan Maclean, at that time the incantation and sacrificial priest, stood with his assistant, Lachlain Maclean, both men of a determined and unbending character, of a powerful build of body, and both unmarried.

Allan Maclean continued his sacrifice to the fourth day, when he was exhausted both in body and mind, and sunk in a swoon; but from this day he received the second-sight to the time of his death, like his assistant. In the people, the belief was unshaken that the second-sight was the natural consequence of celebrating the Taigheirm.

'The infernal spirits appeared, some in the early progress of the sacrifices, in the shape of black cats. The first who appeared during the sacrifice, after they had cast a furious glance at the sacrificer, said — Lachlain Oer, that is, "Injurer of Cats." — Allan, the chief operator, warned Lachlain, whatever he might see or hear, not to waver, but to keep the spit incessantly turning. At length the cat of monstrous size appeared; and after it had set up a horrible howl, said to Lachlain Oer, that if he did not cease before their largest brother came he would never see the face of God. Lachlain answered that he would not cease till he had finished his work if all the devils in hell came. At the end of the fourth day, there sat on the end of the beam in the roof of the barn a black cat with fire-flaming eyes, and there was heard a terrific howl quite across the straits of Mull into Morven.' Allan was wholly exhausted on the fourth day, from the horrible apparitions, and could only utter the word 'Prosperity.' But Lachlain, though the younger, was stronger of spirit, and perfectly self-possessed. He demanded posterity and wealth. And each of them received that which he had asked for. When Allan lay on his death-bed, and his Christian friends pressed around him, and bade him beware of the stratagems of the devil, he replied with great courage, that if Lachlain Oer, who was already dead, and he, had been able a little longer to have carried their weapons, they would have driven Satan himself from his throne, and, at all events, would have caught the best birds in his kingdom.

When the funeral of Allan reached the churchyard, the persons endowed with the second-sight saw at some distance Lachlain Oer, standing fully armed at the head of a host of black cats, and every one could perceive the smell of brimstone which streamed from those cats. Allan's effigy, in complete armour, is carved on his tomb, and his name is yet linked with the memory of the Taigheirm.

J ENNEMOSER,
History of Magic vol II (1854)

WITCHES AS CATS (I)

The association of witches with cats is of great antiquity. In the legends of Greece and Rome, we are told of a woman, who had been changed into a cat, being chosen as priestess by Hecate, the goddess of sorcery and magic power, and of Hecate herself, when the gods were forced to hide themselves in animals, taking refuge in the shape of a cat. The association probably arose not so much from cats being the frequent, almost invariable, companions of the poor old women accused of witchcraft, as from the savage character of the animal itself. Its noiseless and stealthy motions, its persevering watchfulness, its extraordinary agility and tenacity of life, its diabolical caterwauling, prowling habits, deceitful spring, and the luminous appearance of its eyes in the dark, would alone suffice to procure it the name of unearthly; but when infuriated, glaring, bristling, and spitting, it forms a vivid representation of a perfect demon. In the Highlands, it was not, as in the witchcraft of the sixteenth and seventeenth centuries, looked upon as the familiar or attendant imp of the witch, but merely as an animal, whose form witches frequently assumed.

There were other superstitions connected with the animal. Were it not for the fear of being swallowed by the ground, a cat would run much faster than it does. When people have a cat along with them in a boat, they cannot, or will not, be drowned by witches. By burying a cat alive, people waiting for a favourable wind get a breeze from the direction in which its head is put; and a witch, that is, a young one, who is courted by a sailor, can detain him with contrary winds as long as she likes by shutting up the cat in the cupboard. A cat scraping is a sign that some beast, horse, cow, pig, or dog will be found dead on the farm before long. A cat washing its face portends rain next day, and turning its back to the fire storm and rain. When removing from one house to another (*imrich*), it is unlucky to take a cat. The animal was disliked by the MacGregors, and the Camerons of Glenevis could not tolerate it at all.

A shepherd in Kintail, living alone in a bothy, far from other houses, after kindling in the evening a bright cheerful fire, threw himself on a heather bed on the opposite side of the house. About twenty cats entered and sat round the fire, holding up their paws and warming themselves. One went to the window, put a black cap on its head, cried 'Hurrah for London!' and vanished. The other cats, one by one, did the same. The cap of the last fell off, and the shepherd caught it, put it on his own head, cried 'Hurrah for London!' and followed. He reached London in a twinkling, and with his companions went to drink wine in a cellar. He got drunk and fell asleep. In the morning he was caught, taken before a judge, and sentenced to be hanged. At the gallows he entreated to be allowed to wear the cap he had on in the cellar; it was a present from his mother, and he would like to die with it on. When it came the rope was round his neck. He clapped the cap on his head; and cried 'Hurrah for Kintail!' He disappeared with the gallows about his neck, and his friends in Kintail, having by this time missed him, and being assembled in the bothy prior to searching the hills, were much surprised at his strange appearance.

This is a fair specimen of the popular tale. It forms the foundation of the Ettrick Shepherd's 'Witch of Fife.' In Skye, the adventure was claimed by a man nicknamed 'Topsy-turvy' (*But-ar-scionn*) as having occurred to himself. After coming home, he made the gallows into a weaver's loom. The hero in Argyllshire made it the stern and keel of a boat, which may be seen in Lorn to this day. In Harris the hero is a tailor: and the tale has been even found in the Monach isles, west of Uist.

Captain Burt (1730) tells a story of a similar kind which he had heard from a minister. A laird, whose wine was disappearing mysteriously, suspecting witches one night, when he thought the plunderers were at work, entered the cellar, closed the door, and laid about him with a broadsword. When light was brought, the cats, whose eyes he had seen glaring at him in the dark, disappeared, and only some blood was found on the floor. An old woman in the neighbourhood, suspected of being a witch, was found, on her house being entered, in bed, with her leg cut off and lying below the bed. The same story is told of the witches of Thurso (*Inbher-Eòrsa*).

A tailor, named Macilduinn, was left in a house alone on Hallowe'en night, while the rest of the household went to a neighbour's house to hold the festivities of the evening. As he sat on a bed, working at his trade, a great many cats came in, and attacking a bag of flesh at the end of the bed soon tore it up and devoured it. They then gathered round the tailor. One said, 'The back of my paw to Macilduinn!' Another said, 'The front of my paw to Macilduinn!' (*Cùl* a's *aghaidh mo spòige ri Macillduinn*). These threats were repeated by all the rest, while they held out their horrid claws, some derisively, some menacingly, to the poor tailor. Frightened from his wits, he blew out the light, sprung to the door, and took to his heels. The cats gave chase, and by the time he reached a neighbour's house his back was scratched into shreds and thongs (*na iallun*) by the claws of the infernal cats.

Cameron of Doïni, or Glenevis, was out hunting, and killed a wild-cat. The animal, when expiring, asked him to tell, when he went home, that 'the King of the Cats' (*Righ nan Cat*) was dead, or according to others 'the Key of Battle' (*an Iuchair Chath*), or 'the streaked Brindled one' (*a Bhruchail Bhreac*). As he told his story, the little black kitten in the ash-hole (*an toll na luath*) bristled up and swelled, till it was as large as a dog. Cameron said, 'You are swelling, cat.' The cat answered, 'My feathers and my swellings are growing bigger with the heat,' (*Tha m'iteagun's m'atagun ag atadh ris na h-eibhleagun*) and, springing at the chieftain's throat, killed him. The scions of this family (*Teaghlach Dhomhainnidh no Ghliun-Ibheis*) till quite recent times, would not tolerate a cat in the house, from the memory of this tradition.

The same story is told in the following manner, without any locality being assigned for the incident. A hunter killed a wild-cat, and when he came home told his adventure. He said,

> To-night has well prospered with us,
> The big urchal-erchal has been slain.

A kitten that was listening rose and said, 'Has Bald Entrails of the Cats been killed? If it were not the many nights I have got meat and milk in your family, I would have your long brindled weasand in my claws. Tell Streaked Foul-Face, that Bladrum is dead,'[1] and saying this the kitten went away, and was never seen afterwards.

---

[1] ''Sann a nochd a thorchanaich leinn
Mharbhadh an urchuill earchaill mhòr.'
'An do mharbhadh Maol Meanachan nan cat? Mar bhi na h-uile oidhche fhuair mi biadh 'us bainne na d'theaglach, bhiodh do sgòrnan fada riabhach ann am inein. Innis do Bhruc Riabhach gun d'eug Bladrum.'

Near Vaul in Tiree, a man riding home at night, with his son, a young boy, seated behind him, was met by a number of cats. The boy had his hands clasped round his father, and the man, pressing them to his sides, to make surer of the boy's hold, urged his horse to its speed. The cats sprang, and, fastening on the boy, literally devoured him. When the man reached home, with his horse at full gallop, he had only the boy's arms left.

A woman detected a strange cat drinking the milk in her kirn, caught it by the back of the neck, and rapped its nose against the floor. It went about mewing in a melancholy manner, till the woman took pity on it, and called it, saying, 'Puss, puss, till you get a drop' (*Puis, puis, gus am faigheadh tu diar*). The cat answered, 'It is not a drop I want, but the way my mouth is, Mary' (*Cha-ne diar tha mi'g iarraidh ach mar tha mo bhial a Mhàiri*). It then went away, but came back through the night with two other cats. One said they would take the back of their paws to the woman, but the second said the front of their paws. This resolution was carried by the casting vote of the injured cat, and the woman was torn in shreds.

A man, going in the evening to see a girl he was courting, was met at a lonely part of the road (near the end of Balefetrish Hill in Tiree) by seven cats, and was so terrified that he turned back and thereby lost his sweetheart. She married an old man from the village of Hianish, where a noted witch dwelt. The old man got the blame of bribing the witch to send the cats.

In olden times a cat belonging to the tenant of Heynish in Tiree was much addicted, like the rest of its kind, to stealing cheese. It was caught in the act, and, as a punishment for the past and a lesson for the future, its ears were taken off. The tenant had occasion to go from home, and on his return found the cat lying dead, having been hung for theft in his absence. He took it in his lap, and thus addressed it:

> Did I not tell you, little Duncan,
> You had needs of being wary;
> When you went where the cheeses were,
> The gallows would teach you how to dance.
> Evil is it, earless cat,
> They you have killed, because of cheese;
> Your neck has paid for that refreshment,
> At this time, after your death.

On hearing these expressions of sympathy, the cat began to revive, and the man went on:

> A hundred welcomes wait you, cat,
> Since in my lap you've chanced to be;
> And, though I do not much liberty allow,
> Many have you greatly loved.
> Are you the untamed cat that Fionn had,
> That hunted wild from glen to glen?
> Had Oscar you at the battle of Bla-sguinn,
> And left you heroes wounded there?
> You drank the milk Catherine had,
> For entertaining minstrel and meeting;
> And why should I praise you?
> You ought to be, like any kitten,
> On the hill-side seeking mice,
> 'Neath greyish grassy stems and bramble bushes.

On hearing this the cat ran away and was never again seen.

A Tiree boat was tacking out of a loch in the north. A man met it at a point of land near which it came, and asked to be taken to the other side. One of the boatmen was willing, but the rest were not, as they would thereby lose time. Next tack back, the man met the boat again, with the same result. 'Well, then,' he said, 'perhaps you will repent it.' At the mouth of the loch the boatmen heard a howling as of innumerable cats. A storm arose, and with difficulty they reached shelter at the island of Eigg.

J G CAMPBELL,
Witchcraft and Second Sight in the Highlands and Islands of Scotland, 1902

WITCHES AS CATS (II)

When we wold goe in the liknes of an cat, we say thryse ower

> I sall goe in till ane catt,
> With sorrow, and sych, and a blak shot!
> And I shall goe in the Divellis nam,
> Ay quill I com hom again!

And quhen we wold be owt of these shaps, we say

> Cat, catt, God send thee a blak shott!
> I was a catt just now
> Bot I sal be in a woman's liknes evin now.
> Catt, catt, God send thee a blak shot!
> (Pitcairn III, 607–8)

Thus Isobel Gowdie of Auldcarne at her trial in 1662, giving the spell for changing shape into a cat — the formulas for other animals are also given; Robert Graves in *The White Goddess* has reconstructed the whole spell (1961 edn., p 402). In fact, shape-shifting is one of the commonest attributes of the Scottish witch. At Alloa in 1658 Margaret Duchall describes the witches as 'turned all in the liknes of cattis'. Marie Lamont confessed in 1662 that she, 'Kettie Scot, and Margrat Holm, cam to Allan Orr's house in the likenesse of kats' and again that 'the devil turned them in likeness of kats, by shaking his hands above their heads' (quoted in Margaret Murray, *The Witch-Cult in Western Europe*). One of the most mischievous of these cat-witches must have been Isobel Grierson who was burnt in 1607 for having gone into the house of one Adam Clark of Prestonpans in the guise of his cat and accompanied by a great crowd of cats and terrifying his whole family; she also made a habit of visiting another Prestonpans resident, Mr Brown, as a cat and urinating on his wife and all over the house (see C K Sharpe, *An historical account of the belief in witchcraft in Scotland*, 1884, pp 95–6). Sharpe also quotes from the trial of Isobel Young in 1629:

She resett Christian Grinton, a witch, in her house, whom the pannel's husband saw one night to come out at ane hole in the roof, in the likeness of a cat, and theirafter transforme herself in her own likeness: whereupon the pannel told her husband, that it should not faire weill with him, which fell out accordingly; for next day he fell down dead at the pleuch, and was brought hame by the pannel in William Meslet's chaire.

LEWIS CATS

At Torridon, in Wester Ross, there lived in a small house a brother and sister. One evening, before going out to milk, the sister put a salmon on the fire to cook, and told her brother that when he thought the fish quite cooked he was to take it off and put on a pot of potatoes. Just then three strange cats came in, of which one was red and blind of an eye. Moved by pity, the man welcomed them in and began to throw them bits of salmon until nothing was left but the fish bones. After being thus fed, the cats marched to the beach and disappeared in the loch.

Some time after that there was a wonderfully successful herring fishing at Loch Roag on the west of Lewis. Among others who went there was the entertainer of the cats. One night, after he had shot his nets there, he went ashore to look for lodgings. At the first house he entered he was very cordially welcomed by three women, and told that he certainly would get lodgings, and also be well recompensed for previous kindness. In astonishment he asked where they had seen him before. One of them answered, 'Do you not remember when you fed three cats and warmed them at Torridon?' 'Yes,' he said, 'I cannot forget that day, but what do you know about it?' 'I know this, that the three cats were my two companions and myself.' After he had made their further acquaintance, they told him that they went to Torridon to chase herring into the nets of their friends fishing there, and for that purpose assumed the form of whales, but when they wished to land they assumed the form of cats and went to his house, where they received so much kindness.

A VICIOUS CAT

In illustration of the saying that there is no fury in hell like a woman scorned, the following tale is told. A handsome young doctor, for health reasons, went to spend a quiet holiday in a shepherd's house in a remote part of Scotland. The shepherd was pretty old, but his wife was young and handsome, and she soon fell in love with her boarder, and one day disclosed her feelings. He was surprised, and showed his non-appreciation rather strongly. When she saw this she bethought her of how to be avenged for the slight. That night he had horrid dreams, awoke as from a nightmare, and next morning noticed that there was a bleeding scratch on his neck. On the following night he had another nightmare, awoke with a scream, and thought he saw a big black cat jump out at the window. On the following night he took a pistol with him. About midnight he felt unaccountably drowsy. By a great effort of will he managed to waken himself up, got hold of the pistol, and fired at what he believed to be a black cat. The household was aroused, and the wife was found in bed groaning from the pain of a wound in her breast. The matter was explained to the husband, who now knew that she was a witch. The man sent the wife away to the island from which she came, and the matter was hushed up. Long after, the doctor explained how he was nearly done to death by the attempt of the angry witch to inoculate him with some poison.

ALEXANDER POLSON,
Scottish Witchcraft Lore, 1932

THE KING OF THE CATS

CHARLOTTE S BURNE, the daughter of a Herefordshire squire, who contributed this tale to the *Folklore Journal* (vol II, 1884) introduced it as follows: 'When I was a child [*c.* 1845] my father used to tell me the stories of the Kentsham Bell and the King of the Cats, as they were told him by his nurse, who is now living near Ross, and is upwards of ninety years of age.'

Many years ago, long before shooting in Scotland was a fashion as it is now, two young men spent the autumn in the very far north, living in a lodge far from other houses, with an old woman to cook for them. Her cat and her own dogs formed all the rest of the household.

One afternoon the elder of the two young men said he would not go out, and the younger one went alone, to follow the path of the previous day's sport looking for missing birds, and intending to return home before the early sunset. However, he did not do so, and the elder man became very uneasy as he watched and waited in vain till long after their usual supper-time. At last the young man returned, wet and exhausted, nor did he explain his unusual lateness until, after supper, they were seated by the fire with their pipes, the dogs lying at their feet, and the old woman's black cat sitting gravely with half-shut eyes on the hearth between them. Then the young man began as follows:

'You must be wondering what made me so late. I have had a curious adventure to-day. I hardly know what to say about it. I went, as I told you I should, along our yesterday's route. A mountain fog came on just as I was about to turn homewards, and I completely lost my way. I wandered about for a long time, not knowing where I was, till at last I saw a light, and made for it, hoping to get help. As I came near it, it disappeared, and I found myself close to a large oak-tree. I climbed into the branches the better to look for the light, and, behold! it was beneath me, inside the hollow trunk of the tree. I seemed to be looking down into a church, where a funeral was in the act of taking place. I heard singing, and saw a coffin, surrounded by torches, all carried by —— But I know you won't believe me if I tell you!'

His friend eagerly begged him to go on, and laid down his pipe to listen. The dogs were sleeping quietly, but the cat was sitting up apparently listening as attentively as the man, and both young men involuntarily turned their eyes towards him. 'Yes,' proceeded the absentee, 'it is perfectly true. The coffin and the torches were both borne by cats, and upon the coffin were marked a crown and sceptre!' He got no further; the cat started up shrieking, 'By Jove! old Peter's dead! and I'm the King o' the Cats!' rushed up the chimney and was seen no more.

Proverbial Cats

'For he is good to think on, if a man would express himself neatly.'
CHRISTOPHER SMART, on his cat Jeoffrey

Cats are prone to proverbs: they exhibit so many traits characteristic of humans — primarily independence — that from Aesop and Bidpai onwards they have been exploited as examples of both good and bad conduct; Scottish literature and folklore is not lacking in these proverbial cats.

The first collection of Scottish proverbs to be published was James Kelly's *A Complete Collection of Scottish Proverbs . . .* which appeared in 1721. It claimed to explain and make them intelligible to English readers, but they would have had no difficulty in recognising many of them as merely Scotticized versions of English sayings. A selection of those concerning cats has been made. At about the same time in Edinburgh Allan Ramsay was putting together his collections of fables and tales, some of which were original and some taken from the works of la Fontaine and la Motte:

> I'll frae a Frenchman thigg a fable,
>   And busk it in a plaid;
> And tho' it be a bairn of Motte's,
> When I have taught it to speak Scots,
>   I am its second dad.

Fable XI is a neat little parable on justice involving two cats in dispute over a cheese, the matter being decided by 'A monkey with a campsho face, /Clerk to a justice of the peace.'

CAT PROVERBS

1   All Cats are alike grey in the Night.

2   A halfpenny Cat may look at a King.
     An Answer to them that ask you, why you look at them, or what
     you look at.

3   A bleat Cat makes a proud Mouse.
     When Parents and Masters are too mild and easy, it makes their
     Children and Servants too saucy and impertinent.

4   A mufled Cat was never a good Hunter.
     Spoken to them that set about Work with their
     Gloves on.

5   Cats and Carlins sit i' the Sun.
     But fair Maidens sit within.
     Spoken to decoy our Children to sit within, that
     they be not Sun-burn'd.

6   Cast the Cat o'er him.
     It is believed that when a Man is raving in a
     Fever, the Cat cast over him will cure him;
     apply'd to them whom we hear telling
     extravagant Things, as they were raving.

7   Eith to learn the Cat to the Kirn.
     An ill Custom is soon learned,
     but not so soon forgotten.

8   God keep the Cats out of your
    way, for the Hens can flie.
     Spoken with Disdain to them
     that threaten what they will
     do, when we know they dare
     do nothing.

9　I am o'er old a Cat, to draw a Straw before my Nose.

That is, I am too old to be imposed upon. A young Cat will jump at a Straw drawn before her, but not an old one; nothing being more playful than a young Cat, and nothing more dull than an old one.

10　It is well said, but who will bell the Cat.

The Nobility of *Scotland* entered into a Conspiracy against one *Spence*, the Favourite of King *James* the 3ᵈ. It was proposed to go in a Body to *Stirling*, to take *Spence* and hang him, and then to offer their Service to the King as his natural Counsellors. The Lord *Gray* says, *It is well said, but who will bell the Cat*: Alluding to the Fable of the Mice, proposing to put a Bell about the Cat's Neck, that they might be apprised of her coming. The Earl of *Angus* answered, *I will bell the Cat*: Which he effected, and was ever after call'd *Archibald bell the Cat*. The Proverb is us'd when a Thing of great Difficulty is propos'd.

11　It was never for nothing, that the Cat lick'd the Stone.

People who officiously offer their Service, may be Suspected to have some selfish End in it.

Eng. *The Cat knows whose Lips she licks.*

12　No fault but the Cat had a Clean Band, she sets a Bonnet much so weel.

Ironically spoken to them who pretend to do, have, or wear what does not become them.

13　The Cat would fain Fish eat,
But she has no Will to wet her Feet.

Spoken to them that would gladly have, but will not labour.

14　Tine Cat, tine Game.

An Allusion to a Play call'd *Cat i'the Hole*, and the *English* Kit, cat. Spoken when Men at Law have lost their principal Evidence.

15　Well kens the Mouse that the Cat's out of the House.

Eng. *When the Cat's away the Mice will play.*
Lat. *Absente fele, saluint mures.*

16 Wo's them that have the Cat's Dish, and she ay Meuting.
    Spoken when People owe a Thing to, or detain a Thing from
    needy People, who are always calling for it.

17 You'll get no more of the Cat, but the Skin.
    You can have no more of a Person, or Thing, than they can
    afford.

18 You serv'd me as the Wife did the Cat, you cust me in the Kirn
    and hurl'd me out of it.
    Spoken to them that tell us that they relieved us in such a
    Case, alledging that they brought us into it.

19 You never bought Salt to the Cat.
    You know not what it is to provide for a Family.

20 You'll get the Cat with the two Tails.
    A Jest upon People of large Expectations.

from *A Complete Collection of Scottish Proverbs Explained and Made Intelligible
to the English Reader* by JAMES KELLY (1721)

Smudge, the People's Palace cat and her chinas, designed by Margery Clinton and
commissioned by the Friends of the People's Palace, 1986

HANG IN A BOTTLE LIKE A CAT

In his *Reliques of Ancient English Poetry*, referring to the phrase spoken by
Benedick in *Much Ado About Nothing*, 'hang me in a bottle like a cat, and
shoot at me', Bishop Percy notes that 'it is still [1765] a diversion in Scotland
to hang up a cat in a small cask, or firkin, half filled with soot: and then a
parcel of clowns on horseback try to beat out the ends of it, in order to show
their dexterity in escaping before the contents fall upon them.'

A variation of this 'diversion' took place at Haddington in connection
with the May races: the local carters confined a cat in a barrel of soot, hung it
up, and rode at it, attacking it with wooden mallets. (*See* John Martine,
Reminiscences . . . of the County of Haddington, 1890)

And before leaving the subject of cruelty to cats in barrels, here is an
extract from an old chapbook, attributed to the Glasgow bellman Dougal
Graham (1724–1779), 'The Comical Tricks of Lothian Tom'.

> It happened one day that Tom went a fishing, and brought home a few
> small fish, which his grandmother's cat snapt up in the dark. So Tom
> to have justice of the cat for so doing, catches her, and puts her into a
> little tub or cog, then sets her adrift in a small mill-dam, ordering her
> to go a fishing for herself; then set two or three dogs upon her, and a
> most terrible sea fight ensued, as ever was seen on fresh water; for if
> any of the dogs, when attempting to beard her, set up their noses,
> baudrins came flying to that place, to repulse them with her claws;
> then the vessel was like to be overset by the weight of herself, so she
> had to flee to the other, and finding the same there from thence to the
> middle, where she sat mewing, always turning herself about, combing
> their noses with her foot. The old woman being informed of the
> dangerous situation of her dearly beloved cat came running with a long
> poll to beat off the dogs and haul her ashore. What now, says Tom, if
> you be going to take part with my enemies, you shall have part of their
> reward; then gives the old woman such a push that she tumbled into
> the dam over head and ears, beside her beloved cat, and would
> undoubtedly have perished in the water had not one of the people who
> was there looking at the diversion, come to her relief.

THE FOX AND THE CAT

A FABLE

The Fox and the Cat, as they travell'd one day,
With moral discourses cut shorter the way:
' 'Tis great (says the Fox) to make justice our guide!'
'How godlike is mercy!' Grimalkin reply'd.

Whilst thus they proceeded, a Wolf from the wood,
Impatient of hunger, and thirsting for blood,
Rush'd forth as he saw the dull shepherd asleep,
And seiz'd for his supper an innocent Sheep.

'In vain, wretched victim, for mercy you bleat,
When mutton's at hand, (says the Wolf) I must eat.'
Grimalkin's astonish'd, the Fox stood aghast,
To see the fell beast at his bloody repast.
'What a wretch, (says the Cat) 'tis the vilest of brutes:
Does he feed upon flesh, when there's herbage, and roots?'
Cries the Fox, 'While our oaks give us acorns so good,
What a tyrant is this, to spill innocent blood?'

Well, onward they march'd, and they moraliz'd still,
'Till they came where some poultry pick'd chaff by a mill;
Sly Reynard survey'd them with gluttonous eyes,
And made (spite of morals) a pullet his prize.

A Mouse too, that chanc'd from her covert to stray,
The greedy Grimalkin secur'd as her prey.

A Spider that sat in her web on the wall,
Perceiv'd the poor victims, and pity'd their fall;
She cry'd, 'Of such murders how guiltless am I!'
So ran to regale on a new taken fly.

MORAL

The faults of our neighbours with freedom we blame,
But tax not ourselves, tho' we practise the same.

JOHN CUNNINGHAM,
Poems, Chiefly Pastoral, 2nd edn, 1771

THE TWA CATS AND THE CHEESE

Twa *Cats* anes on a *Cheese* did light,
To which baith had an equal Right;
But Disputes, sic as aft arise,
Fell out a sharing of the Prize.
Fair Play, said ane, ye bite o'er thick,
Thae Teeth of your's gang wonder quick:
Let's part it, else lang or the Moon
Be chang'd, the *Kebuck* will be done.
But wha's to do't; — they're Parties baith,
And ane may do the other Skaith,
Sae with Consent away they trudge,
And laid the *Cheese* before a Judge:
A *Monkey* with a champsho Face,
Clerk to a Justice of the Peace,
A Judge he seem'd in Justice skill'd,
When he his Master's Chair fill'd;
Now Umpire chosen for Division,
Baith sware to stand by his Decision.
Demure he looks. — The *Cheese* he pales, —
He prives it good, — Ca's for the Scales;
His Knife whops throw't, — in twa it fell;
He puts ilk haff in either Shell:
Said he, We'll truly weigh the Case,
And strictest Justice shall have Place;
Then lifting up the Scales, he fand
The tane bang up, the other stand:
Syne out he took the heaviest haff,
And ate a Knoost o't quickly aff,
And try'd it syne; — and now prov'd light:
Friend Cats, said he, we'll do ye right.
Then to the ither haff he fell,
And laid till't teughly Tooth and Nail,
Till weigh'd again it lightest prov'd.
The Judge wha this sweet Process lov'd,
Still weigh'd the Case, and still ate on,
'Till Clients baith were weary grown,
And tenting how the Matter went,

Cry'd, Come, come, Sir, we're baith content.
Ye Fools, quoth he, and *Justice* too,
Maun be content as well as you.
Thus grumbled *they*, thus *he* went on,
Till baith the Haves were near hand done:
Poor *Pousies* now the Daffine saw
Of gawn for Nignyes to the Law;
And bill'd the Judge, that he wad please
To give them the remaining Cheese:
To which his Worship grave reply'd,
The Dues of Court maun first be paid.
Now Justice pleas'd: — What's to the fore
Will but right scrimply clear your Score;
That's our Decreet; — gae hame and sleep,
And thank us ye're win aff sae cheap.

ALLAN RAMSAY, *Poems*, 1728

MARISCAT
(For H W)

— What cat is that? — That is a mariscat.
— Cat it is not: it is but a mascot.
— Try it: set it down here at the wainscot.
— *Ceci n'est pas une pipe*. Don't give me scat!
— A wainscot made of words is wondrous wise.
Its mice have holes no millimetrees high.
Its chinks have cheese you cannot breed or buy.
Its cat stalks, purrs, sleeps under paper skies.
Look how the wainscot's in a catmint bed,
the walls have crumbled and the noon's on fire,
the cat is rolling drunk on catmint fumes,
the mice are dancing, their waistcoats are red
with brick-dust and that red will never tire
of warming all these absences of rooms.

EDWIN MORGAN,
Sonnets from Scotland

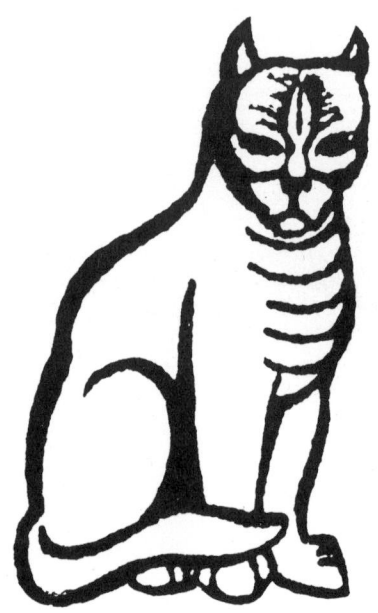

WILDCATS

'these last pure spirits of our dwindling wild places'
MIKE TOMKIES

The Scottish Wildcat, *Felis silvestris grampia*, is one of the most argued about of native British fauna: whether it is tameable; whether it interbreeds with domestic cats and if it does to what extent, and is there a pure breed of wildcat still in Scotland? — these questions are still debated among naturalists: even those who, like David Stephen and Mike Tomkies, have reared wildcats from infancy have differing opinions, on their tameability for example.

The wildcat has been around in Britain for a long time, as fossils of the Pleistocene age found in Essex and elsewhere testify; it now survives in Scotland only, having been driven out of England and Wales by continual hunting and the clearance of woodland for timber and grazing, until by the beginning of the nineteenth century it was practically extinct south of the Tweed.

The Scottish wildcat is thought to be one of the seven sub-species of European wildcat which probably evolved in Europe and Asia from the extinct ancestral species, *Felis lunensis*. The first general description occurs in Konrad von Gesner's *Historia Animalium* (1551–58). Here is James Aikman's description from *The Animal Kingdom* (1861): 'Its usual length is about three feet, including a thick tail of eleven inches. Its colours vary, but the most frequent are yellowish or blackish-grey, and the sides brindled with dark bands.'

For those who wish to read further than this necessarily short selection of extracts, there is an excellent summary (and bibliography) of the history and habits of the wildcat, with the controversies examined, in Mike Tomkies's *My Wilderness Wildcats* (1977), probably the best book there is on the subject. Despite years of being hunted by sportsmen like St John and Thornton or gamekeepers protecting the grouse moors, the number of wildcats seems to be increasing. However, they are still sufficiently rare, especially if, as Mike Tomkies believes, notwithstanding the probability of interbreeding, there is a pure breed surviving in inaccessible areas of the Highlands: he makes a plea for special protection laws — as there already exist in Spain, Germany, and Czechoslovakia.

This section comprises a selection of writings about the Scottish wildcat from the seventeenth century to the present. It begins with the description given in *Scotia illustrata sive Prodomus historiae naturalis*, 1684, by Sir Robert Sibbald (1641–*c*.1712), Professor of Medicine at Edinburgh University, naturalist, and antiquary. It includes an account, in common with most of the early descriptions of cats and wildcats, of the medicinal properties of the animal.

FELIS SYLVESTRIS

Felis Sylvestris major est Domestica, densiore & longiore pilo, colore fusco, variato, cauda crassiore. Aviculis vescitur, Lepusculis, etc.

Cati Sylvestris Axungia calefacit, emollit, discutit. Ad contractus & Articulorum affectur reponitur.

Pellis mollis et pinguiuscula paratur a Pellionibus, ad calefaciendum Ventriculum frigidum appetitumque excitandum, instar Scuti Stomachii. Arthritici Articulis imponunt.

The wildcat is larger than the domestic cat, its fur is thicker and longer, yellowish in colour, brindled, with a thicker tail. It feeds on small birds and young hares, etc.

Its fat or grease has warming, softening and dispersive properties. It is applied in the restoring of contractions and afflictions of the joints.

Its soft and fatty pelt is prepared by furriers for warming the cold belly and stimulating the appetite, like a stomach shield. Arthritis sufferers put it on their joints.

Sir ROBERT SIBBALD,
Scotia illustrata sive Prodomus historiae naturalis, 1684

The Wild Cat (*Felis catus*)

WILDCATS OF BADENOCH

Thomas Thornton (1757–1823) of Thornville in Yorkshire, was educated at Charterhouse and Glasgow University, and it was while he was in Glasgow that he 'manifested a passion for field sports, especially hawking, on which he expended much time and money, resolving to bring the sport as near perfection as possible.' (J Harting, *Bibliotheca Accipitraria*, 1891)

A sporting tour through . . . the Highlands was not published until 1804, although the actual tour took place probably in 1786. By his own account Thornton seems to have been a greater menace to Highland game than any wildcat; it is difficult not to agree with Sir Walter Scott (himself by no means opposed to blood sports) who reviewed the book thus: 'a long, minute and prolix account of every grouse or black-cock which had the honour to fall by the guns of our literary sportsman — of every pike which gorged his bait — of every bird which was pounced by his hawks — of every blunder which was made by his servants — and of every bottle which was drunk by himself and his friends.'

September 4 . . . The dogs, in the course of this day, got upon something, I could not tell what, which they footed a considerable way, and by the bristles rising on their backs, I plainly perceived it was not game but vermine. Conceived it to be a wild cat, or martin, which, in these moors abound, and should have been particularly pleased to have got a shot at it, but it escaped me.

The wild cats here are very large, nearly the bulk of a middling-sized fox, remarkably fierce, and very destructive to game and lambs. Their brush is nearly as thick as that of the fox.

Colonel THOMAS THORNTON, *A sporting tour
through the northern parts of England and great part
of the Highlands of Scotland* (1804)

A SUTHERLAND WILDCAT

The true wild cat is gradually becoming extirpated, owing to the increasing preservation of game; and though difficult to hold in a trap, in consequence of its great strength and agility, he is by no means difficult to deceive, taking any bait readily, and not seeming to be as cautious in avoiding danger as many other kinds of vermin. Inhabiting the most lonely and inaccessible ranges of rock and mountain, the wild cat is seldom seen during the day time; at night (like its domestic relative) he prowls far and wide, walking with the same deliberate step, making the same regular and even track, and hunting its game in the same tiger-like manner; and yet the difference between the two animals is perfectly clear, and visible to the commonest observer. The wild cat has a shorter and more bushy tail, stands higher on her legs in proportion to her size, and has a rounder and coarser look about the head. The strength and ferocity of the wild cat when hemmed in or hard pressed are perfectly astonishing. The body when skinned presents quite a mass of sinew and cartilage. I have occasionally, though rarely, fallen in with these animals in the forests and mountains of this country; once, when grouse-shooting, I came suddenly, in a rough and rocky part of the ground, upon a family of two old ones and three half-grown young ones. In the hanging birch-woods that border some of the Highland streams and lochs, the wild cat is still not uncommon, and I have heard their wild and unearthly cry echo far in the quiet night as they answer and call to each other. I do not know a more harsh and unpleasant cry than that of the wild cat, or one more likely to be the origin of superstitious fears in the mind of an ignorant Highlander. These animals have great skill in finding their prey, and the damage they do to the game must be very great, owing to the quantity of food which they require. When caught in a trap, they fly without hesitation at any person who approaches them, not waiting to be assailed. I have heard many stories of their attacking and severely wounding a man, when their escape has been cut off. Indeed, a wild cat once flew at me, in the most determined manner. I was fishing at a river in Sutherlandshire, and in passing from one pool to another had to climb over some rock and broken kind of ground. In doing so, I sank through some rotten heather and moss up to my knees, almost upon a wild cat, who was concealed under it. I was quite as much startled as the animal herself could be, when I saw the wild-looking beast so unexpectedly rush out from between my feet, with every hair on her body standing on end, making her look twice as large as she really was. I had three small Skye terriers with me, who immediately gave chace, and pursued her till she took refuge in a corner of the rocks, where, perched in a kind of recess out of reach of her enemies, she stood with her hair bristled out, and spitting and growling like a common cat. Having no weapon with me, I laid down my rod, cut a good-sized stick, and proceeded to dislodge her. As soon as I was within six or seven feet of the place, she sprang straight at my face over the dogs' heads. Had I not struck her in mid air as she leaped at me, I should probably have got some severe wound. As it was, she fell with her back half broken amongst the dogs, who, with my assistance, dispatched her. I never saw an animal fight so desperately, or one which was so difficult to kill. If a tame cat has nine lives, a wild cat must have a dozen. Sometimes one of these animals takes up its residence at no great distance from a house, and entering the hen-house and outbuildings, carries off fowls or even lambs in the most audacious manner. Like other vermin, the wild cat haunts the shores of the lakes and rivers, and it is therefore easy to know where to lay a trap for them. Having caught and killed one of the colony, the rest of them are sure to be taken if the body of their slain relative is left in some place not far from their usual hunting-ground, and surrounded with traps, as every wild cat who passes within a considerable distance of the place will to a certainty come to it. The same plan may be adopted successfully in trapping foxes, who also are sure to visit the dead body of any other fox which they scent during their nightly walk. There is no animal more destructive than a common house-cat, when she takes to hunting in the woods. In this case they should always be destroyed, and when once they have learned to prefer hares and rabbits to rats and mice, they are sure to hunt the larger animals only. I believe, however, that by cropping their ears close to the head, cats may be kept from hunting, as they cannot bear the dew and rain to enter these sensitive organs. Tame cats who have once taken to the woods soon get shy and wild, and then produce their young in rabbit-holes, decayed trees, and other quiet places; thus laying the foundation of a half-wild race. It is worthy of notice, that whatever colour the parents of these semi-wild cats may have been, those bred out of them are almost invariably of the beautiful brindled grey colour, as the wild cats. A shepherd, whose cat had come to an untimely end — by trap or gun, I forget which — in lamenting her death to me, said it was a great pity so valuable an animal should be killed, as she brought him every day in the year either a grouse, a young hare, or some other head of game. Another man told me that his cat brought to the house during the whole winter a woodcock or a snipe almost every night, showing a propensity for hunting in the swamps and wet places near which the cottage was situated, and where these birds were in the habit of feeding during the night. A favourite cat of my own once took to bringing home rabbits and hares, but never winged game. Though constantly caught in traps, she could never be cured of her hunting propensities. When caught in an iron trap, instead of springing about and struggling, and by this means breaking or injuring her legs, she used to sit quietly down and wait to be let out. There is a cat at the farm now, who is caught at least twice a week, but from adopting the same plan of waiting quietly and patiently to be liberated, she seldom gets her foot much hurt.

CHARLES ST JOHN, *Short Sketches of the Wild Sports and Natural History of the Highlands* (1846)

THE WILDCAT OF EUROPE

Edward Hamilton's book, *The Wild Cat of Europe*, 1896, was the first to bring together the various descriptions, theories, and observations concerning the wildcat; what sparked off the work was his surprise at a well-known naturalist admitting almost total ignorance of the wildcat — the only example, as Hamilton says, of the Feline family indigenous to Britain. He finally came to the conclusion that 'It would seem as if the original Wild Cat, as it existed in the olden days, has been almost exterminated throughout Europe, and that its place has been taken by a mongrel race, the result of continual interbreeding'. Hamilton produces documentary evidence on the wildcat as found in various parts of Europe, from the earliest records to the latest: the following extracts are from the chapter on Scotland.

BINGLEY, writing in 1809, says that 'in the united parishes of Loch Goil Head and Kilmorich in Argyleshire, Wild Cats are more numerous than Foxes, and will at times, especially when wounded, attack human beings.'

Sir WALTER SCOTT, writing in 1824 ('Familiar Letters,' 1893), states that the gardener at Lochore in Fifeshire, one John Macleod, told him that he had destroyed, of vermin, two Wild Cats, eight household Cats gone wild, five Polecats, one of terrible size and weight, which Sir Walter thinks must have been a Marten Cat, five Weasels, three Whitretts, besides sundry Magpies.

SELBY ('Quadrupeds and Birds of the County of Sutherland,' 1835) states that the Wild or Mountain Cat is very plentiful in the mountain districts, where they attain a great size, and at times commit great ravages upon the young lambs in Assynt; upon the Ben More range they are very numerous, and find secure shelter and protection in the numerous caverns and holes in the limestone districts.

MACGILLIVRAY (Nat. Libr. vol. ii. 1838) says that the Wild Cat appears to be more abundant in the woods of the counties of Perth, Aberdeen, and Argyle than in any other part of Scotland, and specimens from these districts are not unfrequently sent to Edinburgh to be preserved.

The same author, writing in 1855, reports that the Wild Cat had become extremely rare.

ROBERT GRAY, in a list of the Quadrupeds of Loch Lomond and its vicinity, in 1877, states that this undoubted species has been repeatedly trapped in the immediate vicinity of the Loch.

The late E R ALSTON ('The Fauna of Scotland,' 1880) says that this animal, once generally distributed over the mainland, is not totally extirpated in the lowlands and in many parts of the highlands. It is still to be found, however, in the wilder districts of most of the northern counties, especially in the Deer forests, where it is left comparatively undisturbed. Till of late years its southern outpost was the mountainous country about Loch Lomond; but it is now extinct in that neighbourhood, and Alston believed that none exist south of the northern district of Argyle and Perthshire. There appears to be no evidence that the Wild Cat was ever found in any of the Islands.

J A HARVIE-BROWN, in 'The Past and Present Distribution of the Rarer Animals of Scotland' (Zool. 1881), gives a list of the different counties in which the Wild Cat has been killed or last seen in the present century. He states that in Dumfries, Kirkcudbrightshire, and Wigtonshire not one has been seen for the last 50 years. The last traditional Wild Cat in the museum at Dumfries proved on close inspection to be an unusually finely stuffed example of the common Tabby. The last Wild Cat killed in Dunbartonshire was in 1857, in Stirlingshire in 1842. In Perthshire, where formerly it was abundant, a correspondent informs Harvie-Brown that an example of the Wild Cat has not been seen for the last twenty years, and adds that many so-called Wild Cats have been proved to be, on close examination, Domestic Cats which had taken to the woods.

In Forfarshire and Kincardineshire there is no record since 1850. In Aberdeenshire the last reported was in 1877, and in Banff, Elgin, and Nairn no record for the last fifty years. In some parts of Inverness-shire, Harvie-Brown states that it is still found about Arisaig and Moidart on the west coast, and in Lochaber and on Ben Alder further inland.

In Argyleshire a Wild Cat was killed in 1879, near Strontian House, Sunart, and one was taken alive at Ranachan, in Camusain Wood, on the north side of Loch Sunart. A correspondent stated to Harvie-Brown that in 1875 'the lady of a neighbouring proprietor applied to me for assistance in procuring from fifteen to twenty Wild Cat skins for a lining to a gentleman's "dreadnought" or ulster. In a few weeks, by purchase or otherwise, the requisite number was obtained. Most were, no doubt, killed between 1872 and 1875, and were procured from the districts of Arisaig, Moidart, Ardnamurchan, Sunart, Ardgour, and Morvern.'

This has since been proved to be quite incorrect. They were the skins of Crofters' cats, common house tabbies, all very fine and large, and it is more than probable that most of the Wild Cats reported as genuine Wild Cats for the last fifty years have the same origin. Four very fine examples of the mixed breed have been taken within the last year, 1895–6, in Morvern, Argyleshire — the tails very thick, the rings and tip black.

The same author, writing in 1881, considers that the Wild Cat has become almost, if not entirely, extinct, all south and east of a line commencing, roughly speaking, at Oban, continuing north-west of the junction of the three counties of Perth, Forfar, and Aberdeen, thence across the corner of the Dee to Tomintoul, Banff, to the city of Inverness.

Further north Messrs HARVIE-BROWN and T E BUCKLEY ('A Vertebrate Fauna of Sutherland, Caithness, and Cromarty') state that, although it has become extremely rare in Assynt, it is said to be found in the Forest of Reay; but in answer to an application we made for an example from that forest in November 1891, the Duke of Westminster wrote:— 'The genuine Wild Cat is, as you know, a very rare animal indeed, and I do not know of any in the Reay country, but will write down and enquire, and if there is such a thing and it can be got you shall have it.'

The Wild Cat is not found on any of the islands of the Outer and Inner Hebrides. The examples reported from Skye, Mull, Gigha, Canna, &c. are the offspring of the Crofters' cats run wild, a very common occurrence in all parts of the Highlands and elsewhere.

Messrs HARVIE-BROWN and T E BUCKLEY ('A Fauna of the Outer Hebrides'), under the heading of Wild Cat, give the following observations, proving how much care is necessary in taking the reports of keepers and others as to the existence of the Wild Cat in the Hebrides; and these remarks apply equally to the reports of the presence of Wild Cats in many other districts besides North Britain:

'Of many entries of "Wild Cats" in the very complete list of vermin killed between 1876 and 1885 inclusive (furnished by the courtesy of the Chamberlain of the Lews, Mr W Mackay) not one can be held as applicable to the true wild species; and we mention this here in order to set up a guide-post to others in all future collections of similar statistics. The said records present a steadily increasing crop of cats averaging 28·7 (*sic*) for ten years, there being 30 killed in 1876 and 41 in 1885; now from all the records of true Wild Cats that we possess (and of these we have a large number from many parts of Scotland) such an increase is most unlikely, if not actually impossible, and besides our own observations, we have a still higher authority in the late Mr E R Alston, all pointing to the fact that *Felis catus* has not existed in the Outer Hebrides within historic times.'

EDWARD HAMILTON,
The Wildcat of Europe, 1896

Hamilton and others at the turn of the century felt that the wildcat was on the point of extinction — hunted and trapped almost out of existence — but since then the situation has improved: the two World Wars gave the wildcat some respite from hunters and the Forestry Commission's widespread planting offered new cover. The position up to the present can be seen below.

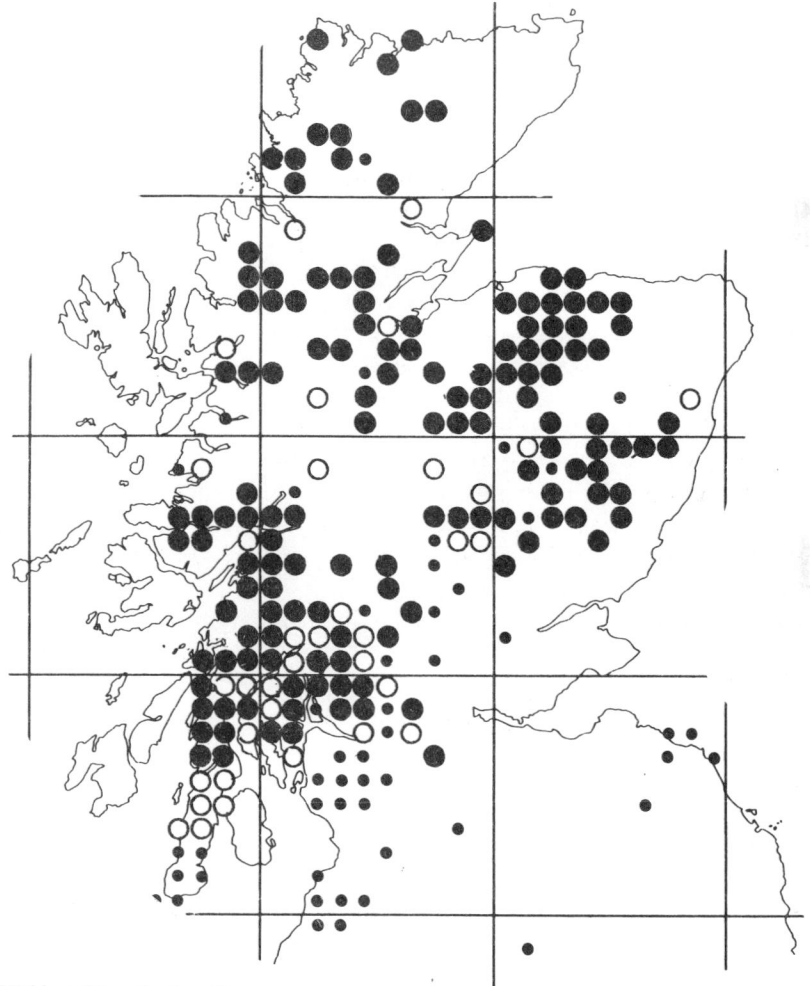

Wildcat Distribution Map

Each symbol refers to at least a single sighting or record from tracks or feeding remains and in some cases several records or sightings. Detailed evidence was required before sightings were accepted, so feral domestic cats are not mistakenly recorded. This map was prepared by the Biological Records Centre, Monks Wood Experimental Station, Huntingdon, from records supplied by the Mammal Society.

●   *pre 1900*   ○   *1900–1959*   ●   *1960–1985*

Wildcat and kitten. Dot McIntosh

Here are two pieces by *The Scotsman*'s wildlife correspondent, David Stephen, on wildcats and wild cats (definitely not synonymous). Concerning the latter, there have been many stories, since the early 1970s, of sightings of large, often puma-sized, cats in Scotland. For details of these see Graham J McEwan's *Mystery Animals of Britain and Ireland*, 1986.

THE CALL OF THE WILDCAT

A visitor looking at my big tame wildcat said: He doesn't look very wild to me. These seven words say it all. People have become so brainwashed with the stereotype of the snarling, bristling wildcat that they tend to think the cat never unglues its ears from its skull or locks its teeth away. The wildcat, I tell them, is a species, living wild not bilin wild.

The stereotype is a phoney: an angry cat, a scared cat, a cat at bay, a cornered cat. Yet people are so besotted with the image that no Editor will look at a photograph that shows a happy cat, a contented cat, relaxed and at ease. Of course, when a wildcat bristles and displays all its weaponry of teeth and claws it is a magnificently terrifying sight. But that's the exception.

Ordinarily, it goes about like any other cat — the drawing shows an adult yawning at an obstreporous kitten — although it's like no ordinary cat.

There are plenty of ordinary cats running wild that superficially resemble the real thing; but they can never become wildcats, nor breed wildcats. The wildcat is a species, not a way of life; the wild cat is just a cat living wild.

A big male wildcat will weigh up to 7 kilograms, and a big female up to $5\frac{1}{2}$ kilograms. Big males will measure up to 100cm from nose to tail tip; females up to 75cm. The skull is wide, the ears angled out. But the tail is the sure give-away: it is thick, with black rings, and a blunt black tip.

All domestic cats running wild, whatever their markings, have a long tail tapering to a slender tip.

It is one of the great sounds of nature to hear the wild pibroch of a wildcat on the hill at night; then you'll hear it all — demonic laughter, saw-edged screeches, and eldritch yowls.

One of the most exciting nights I ever spent on the hill was beside an eagle's eyrie, with a wildcat squalling on the rocks above me, on and off during the darkness. Then, in the slanting morning sunlight, I watched it stalking on the scree below — big, muscular, powerful — the wildest of wild things in the wildest of settings.

Unlike the domestic cat, the wildcat does not carry home live prey to kittens. Again, unlike the domestic cat, it does not bury its droppings; in fact they are used as markers on territory. Urine is also used for this purpose, and my big male wildcat never misses an opportunity of spraying me if I stand beside his favourite marking place.

Territory defended by the male cat runs to 70 hectares, according to various authorities, but hunting range is larger than this, especially during winter and the breeding season (from January to June inclusive).

The breeding den may be under a tree root, among rocks, or even in the old eyrie of a golden eagle. The female does all the work of rearing the young. Litter size is usually three or four; more often four. Bigger litters may be the result of interbreeding with domestic cats.

Two litters a year seem to be common in Scotland (my captive pair had produced two litters) and there have been reports of three. But this is based on time of year when kittens were found; and late litters could be firsts or thirds. My own feeling is that triple littering, if it occurs at all, indicates an admixture of domestic blood.

The kittens begin to appear at the den mouth at about four weeks of age, and the mother plays with them a great deal. They are weaned at about four months, and are independent at five months. They are fully grown before they are a year old, and breed in the year following their birth.

Although wildcats sometimes kill big prey, like mountain hares, grouse and blackcocks (even roe deer fawns I am told), their prey is mostly small rodents like voles and woodmice. This is confirmed by studies in continental Europe. In France it was found that 92 per cent of cat stomachs contained voles and 25 per cent contained mice. Yet the wildcat is still slaughtered on grouse moors where (with notable exceptions) everything with a hooked beak or canine teeth goes anyway, grouse moor keepers being, in the main (again with notable exceptions) a peculiarly single-minded and ruthless breed.

The wildcat is supposed to be untameable. It isn't. If hand-reared from infancy it becomes like any domestic cat; if tamed young it remains unpredictable; if taken adult it remains untameable.

DAVID STEPHEN,
The Scotsman, 3 March 1979

MIXED BLOOD IN THE HEATHER

Writing in *The Scotsman* about 30 years ago on the subject of the Scottish wildcat (sometimes written wild-cat or wild cat) I used the phrase: 'You'll sometimes hear the treason whispered that there's no such animal.' I went on from there to discuss the extent of interbreeding between the wildcat and the domestic and the problems this created. The problem is still with us and is presently being tackled by Dr Easterbee of the Nature Conservancy Council.

I thought this might be a good time to do a wee bit of recapitulation.

When is a wildcat not a wildcat? When it's merely a domestic cat that has deserted the fireside and taken to the free life of the hill. It lives the wild life but remains what it was when it left home.

On the hill it may or may not be mated to a wildcat; equally it might be killed by one. The late Dr L H Matthews wrote in 1952: '. . . the crossing has, of course, taken place in two directions and the wildcat has become diluted with domestic cat genes.' The words 'of course' suggested that this was well known. It wasn't.

Matthews also wrote: 'Contrary to the opinion of some writers, there is no indication of any degeneration in the robustness of the wildcat of Scotland when compared with the remains left by its prehistoric ancestors.' Then: 'the general impression found is that a cline exists with an increasing amount of true wildcat genes the farther north one looks.'

What Prof Suminski came up with in 1962 would seem to support this.

Suminski, working on colour and skull formation, tried to show the proportion of characters that are typical wildcat as against others due to hybridisation. The purest wildcats were Polish (73 per cent) followed by Scottish (66 per cent), dropping to 44 per cent for those from the French and Swiss Alps.

Are wildcats smaller than they used to be? The great Ritchie (1920) suggested that wildcats of the Neolithic period were bigger than the present population. The result of hybridisation? Or no more than a general evolutionary trend?

It used to be said that the wildcats of Europe bred only once a year, in May. The Scottish wildcat will breed twice, and sometimes even a third time, and this has been held to indicate a big mixture of domestic blood. This has always struck me as dubious because it suggests that

the European cat avoids miscegenation while the Scottish cat laps it up.

My own wildcats Teuchter and Pibroch produced only one litter a year throughout their breeding life. That begs more questions than it answers.

Here is the best example of cross-mating that I know of. A stalker friend watches his domestic cat go to the hill and tries a rifle shot at the big cat waiting to meet her. Several days later she comes home fit and well. A little over eight weeks later she produces young, which she hides away. Eventually her place is discovered and three kittens are found. I got one of the kittens, whom we call Tosh.

He was a spitting fury about six weeks old who drew blood from anyone who came near him, and I had to handle him with horsehide gloves. It took me seven weeks to tame him, during which period he marked my wife for life. Then he became absurdly tame.

Here was a chance, I thought, to do an experiment in breeding, and I discussed the possibility with Gilbert Fisher of Edinburgh Zoo, who agreed. Unfortunately, a month before the time, I had to flit from Luggiebank and Tosh was killed.

The next hybrid I had was box-trapped when he was about eight weeks old. He was totally unmanageable and was allowed to go back to the hill.

Since then I have had only the real thing. My wife and I reared two kittens in the early seventies. The female's eyes were open and she was a spitfire; the male's eyes were still ungummed and he was tame from the day he opened them. The female is still alive; the male died a few weeks ago.

DAVID STEPHEN,
The Scotsman, 7 March 1987

THE SCOTTISH WILDCAT IN HERALDRY

The novelist C P Snow when he became Baron Snow, may have been having a mild whimsical dig at the Establishment when he adopted domestic cats as supporters for his baronial shield and crest. These are described in Burke's *Peerage* as 'Siamese cats proper' — simply 'cat' with breed designated. The wildcat, which lies in the ranks of heraldic felines somewhere between the ubiquitous rampant lion of Scotland and Snow's elegant oriental aristocrats, attracts a separate distinct designation — the archaic term, 'Cat-o-mountain'.

Felis sylvestris grampia — the Scottish wildcat, is the most ferocious wild animal surviving in this country today and well deserves its reputation as 'the British tiger'. This is the beast which best embodied the spiritual and physical temper desired by the Highland clansmen who adopted it as device. One author on heraldry, describing a coat-of-arms wrote '. . . the cat sejant gardant proper of the Grants of Ballindalloch is no jolly gib but a real cat-o-mountain'. In *The Law and Practice of Heraldry in Scotland* (1863) George Seton notes that people would often incorporate into their blazonry, flowers, birds and beasts which symbolised favoured virtues or desirable talents. So it may be that in addition to its known ferocity, the supposed magical capacity of cats to summon up rains or storms or as harbingers of good fortune, made the wildcat doubly significant as a talisman for the field of battle.

In Scottish heraldry the wildcat holds a worthy position in the hierarchy of osprey, goshawk, ptarmigan, bear, boar, Angus bull and even the dragons of Dundee. There are instances of its occurrence in Celtic blazonry across the Irish Sea where the O'Cahan family carries as crest 'a cat-o-mountain rampant' above the motto *Felis demulcta mitis* (The stroked cat is meek). This could be a fine form of the Irish joke, since the prospect of stroking this notably untameable animal into meekness is a daunting one. It would seem more pertinent to apply the prudent Scottish caution of Clan Chattan which advocates 'Touch not a Cat bot [without] a Glove' on most of its armorial bearings.

The Clan Chattan is a widely ranging confederation of about twenty clans, principally Mackintosh and Macpherson, which originated in the Badenoch area in the thirteenth century. Although *chat* is a form of the Gaelic word for cat and many fine Highland families cherish the

Arms of Clan Mackintosh

notion of descent from the 'race of cat-o-mountain', this seems an
unlikely origin. The more prosaic and widely accepted account is that
the name derives from the first Chief, Gillichattan Mor, who was the
baillie or temporal custodian of the abbey lands of Ardchattan Priory
in Benderloch. Gillies is today one of the family names gathered into
the clan grouping. While other tales of origin linked with Gallic tribes
and the wildcat country of Caithness or 'Catav' (Sutherland) may be
romantically desirable, if apocryphal, the traditional link with the
wildcat remains in the cat-o-mountain on the clan devices and the
warning motto recorded for succeeding chiefs to this day.

When a coat-of-arms is granted by the Lord Lyon, a record is made
in the Register of Arms in the form of a document known as an Extract
of Matriculation of Arms. In Scotland this Register is held at Register
House in Edinburgh. The drafting of the Matriculation documents is
carried out by heraldic artists and they are outstandingly fine examples
of drawing, painting and calligraphy. The interpretation of the
characteristics of particular birds, beasts or fishes, real or monstrous,
owes much to the skills and imagination of these artists.

Some of the Extracts are illustrated in *Scots Heraldry* (1956) by Sir
Thomas Innes of Learney, and Plate XLVI shows the record dated
1947 which confirmed Mackintosh of Mackintosh-Torcastle, Duncan
Alexander Mackintosh as 31st Hereditary Chief of Clan Chattan. This
is a superb piece of work and depicts three wildcats surrounding the
shield; one atop 'salient gardant' as crest and larger animals 'gardant'
on either side of the shield, all three with clubbed tails erect, and claws
and fangs bared with a wild ferocity, ready to gouge out the heart and
lights of any man daring to dispute their supremacy. Perhaps
marginally less splendid and fearsome than Chattan, as befitting a
lesser mortal (but only just), is a similar set of arms, confirmed also
in 1947, with three cats for Rear-Admiral Lachlan Macintosh of
Macintosh, The Macintosh, Chief of Clan Macintosh. This is shown
on Plate XXVIII of the same book.

At one point in Clan Chattan's history towards the end of the
seventeenth century, there was a dispute for overall Chiefship between
the Mackintoshes and Macphersons, this being resolved by the Lyon
Court in favour of Mackintosh. These were the two main clans of the
confederation, and while the victorious Mackintosh arms sport the
three cats described above, the Macpherson arms, perhaps signifi-
cantly, show a more modest 'cat-o-mountain sejant'. This sits as crest
atop the helmet which caps a shield flanked by two bearded clansmen
with sword and targe. In some versions of this blazon the scale of the
cat relative to the warriors gives it the air of a domestic tabby, but
closer examination makes clear the club-ended tail, fangs and claws of

Arms of Madam Myrtle Farquharson of Invercauld

the ready fighter. Another Macpherson cat is to be seen on Plate XVIII of *Scots Heraldry*. In this twentieth century drawing the artist seems at first glance to have imparted a slightly comic air to the wildcat under the Gaelic motto, but this impression is soon dispelled. This is no cartoon cat, he sits arched and alert, tail curved in an incipient thrash, every line of the body daring an ungloved hand.

The product of the heraldic artist's mind and hand may, in some instances, as in other artistic commissions, be subjected to some influence from the client. In Learney's book the coat-of-arms of Madame Myrtle Farquharson of Invercauld, Chief of the Clan in

1936, is illustrated on Plate XXXII. There is a fierce sword-brandishing lion as crest above the lozenge (in lieu of shield for a lady) which is embraced by two decidedly feminine wildcats with finely curving legs, smoothly upswept tails and paws delicately poised on the central element. The expression on the faces of the cats is one of mildly surprised affront at being asked to perform such a task. However, turn to the straight clan arms of Farquharson and one is faced by two beasts with flattened ears, a rictus of aggressive fang, and claws tensioned, ready to take issue with any. The underlying motto here is 'I force nae

Michael Bruce
de la Valle Macpherson

Arms of Michael Bruce de la Valle Macpherson

freen: I fear nae foe' — here is the solo cat-o-mountain coursing the hills and glens, ready to defend offspring and territory to the death.

Artistic interpretation can be further considered in *Fairbairn's Crests* (1905) Volume 1, which catalogues family names and mottoes and illustrates the crest elements of myriad coats-of-arms. The illustrations are gathered in analogous groupings and Plates 25/26 show finely engraved representations of cats, ranging from a sad moggy bearing a staff with Union Jack to a varied range of wildcats; the former, in its fey Irish manner, as emblem for the grand name of Baron Keane of Ghunze in Afghanistan and Cappoquin, Co. Waterford, the latter from a variety of family arms including the Scottish clans. There are cats sejant, cats couchant, rampant, salient and courant, descriptions from the cornucopia of the heraldic lexicon, words redolent of the battlefield and courts of chivalry. The cats are posed on these pages, strangely divorced from the main corpus of

The Arms of the Royal Burgh of Dornoch

helmet, shield, supporters and motto; *in vacuo* as it were, they are sometimes comical, sometimes sad. There is one small head, full face with a mouthful of rodent, a disconsolate looking fellow with singularly uncatlike eyes resembling black marbles, and a sorry beast, 'couped' at the waist, with fur quartered in contrasting colours and brandishing a branch of flowers — an effete activity with which to charge a bold cat-o-mountain.

Flowers and decorated fur were no part of the wildcat's accoutrements in the days when Norse invaders were marauding into Sutherland. A folktale of those early centuries tells how one raider was besieged by a group of wildcats which he vanquished after a fierce and bloody battle. That man became the first Thane of Sutherland. The Gaelic title for the Duke is 'Morair Chat' (The Great Man of the Cats), and he must have been a fearless fighter indeed, in face of the wild aggression displayed by the beast that holds place as crest on the Ducal arms under the motto *Sans Peur*. This motto 'Without Feare' was carried into the twentieth century with the granting of a coat-of-arms to the Royal Burgh of Dornoch in 1929. The town of Dornoch has links with the first Thane, and was created a Royal Burgh in 1628 with some reservation of rights to the Earl of Sutherland, the hereditary superior. This connection is acknowledged in the 1929 arms by the defiant cat under the fearless motto, atop the helmet and shield bearing a horseshoe ('Dorneich' in Gaelic), commemorating the slaying of the Danish general at Embo in 1259, by the Thane wielding a horse's leg seized on the battlefield. A doughty warrior, The Great Man of the Cats.

When traditional and historic lines of demarcation from the centuries were erased in 1975, and modern marches defined, in the bloodless but sometimes controversial cause of more efficient local government, coats-of-arms were devised for the new bureaucracy of the Regional and District Councils. Native flora, fauna and fishes, extant and extinct adorned the heraldic records. This democratic blazonry of the 'posse comitatus' managed to yield a small concession to ancient aristocracy. On the arms granted to Inverness District Council, the Mackintosh cat is placed 'in chief' at the top of the shield.

The cat-o-mountain still quarters the Grampians, the 'British tiger' still springs 'salient proper' on the parchment at Register House.

TOM BERRY

THE WILDCAT

The wildcat sits on the rock.
His hair is spitting fire
into the morning air.
His eyes are yellow.

Club-headed dynamic cat,
he is all power and force.
Among the dry green grass,
the hares are playing.

The air is clear and pure.
The hares are leaping and jumping
over invisible fences
of a pure brilliant blue.

The wildcat sits by himself
on his stony throne, not thinking.
His fur simmers like fire
snarling and sparking.

IAIN CRICHTON SMITH

MUTUAL LIFE

A wildcat, fur-fire in a bracken bush,
Twitches his club-tail, rounds his amber eyes
At rockabye rabbits humped on the world. The air
Crackles about him. His world is a rabbit's size.

And in milky pearls, in a liquefaction of green,
One of ten thousand, spattering squabs of light,
A mackerel shuttles the hanging waterwebs,
Muscling through tons, slipping them left and right.

What do you know, mind, of that speck in air,
The high, insanitary raven that pecks his claws
A thousand feet up and volplanes on his back
And greets his ancient sweetheart with coarse caws?

You tell a hand to rise and you think it yours.
It makes a shape (you have none) in a space
It gives perspective to. You sink in it
And disappear there, foundered without trace.

And dreadful alienations bring you down
Into a proper loneliness. You cry
For limits that make a wildcat possible
And laws that tumble ravens in the sky.

Till clenched hand opens, drowning into you,
Where mackerel, wildcat, raven never fall
Out of their proper spaces; and you are
Perpetual resurrection of them all.

NORMAN MACCAIG

CAT AND MOUSE

Lat take a cat, and fostre hym wel with milk
And tendre flessche, and make his couche of silk,
And let hym seen a mous go by the wal;
Anon he weyvith milk, and flessche, and al,
And every deyntee that is in that hous,
Swich appetyt hath he to ete a mouse.

CHAUCER, 'The Maunciple's Tale'

All the tales and fables recognise the fact that a cat will go to any lengths to catch, toy with, and kill a mouse. However, in most of these that concern the age-old conflict it is the mice who usually win the upper hand, as if to balance the natural course of events — and even when the mouse loses, as in 'The Cameronian Cat', the cat does not escape retribution, here a fate determined by fanatical Scottish Sabbatarianism. The tale of the town mouse and the country mouse is a familiar one, but Henryson's is a splendid Scottish version and features 'Gib Hunter, our Jolie Cat', the first cat, as far as can be determined, to make an appearance in Scottish literature. Alexander Gray's poem is much anthologised, but can bear repetition.

'GIB HUNTER, OUR JOLIE CAT'

Little is known about Robert Henryson, the greatest of the Scottish makars: he was possibly a schoolteacher in Fife. The tale of the two mice is from his *Morall Fabillis*, probably written in the 1470s. It has been suggested that the cat, Gib, in the poem represents James III of Scotland who could well have been thought of as playing with his subjects as the cat toys with the country mouse. For an interesting discussion of this subject, see Robert L Kindrick, 'Lion or Cat? Henryson's Characterization of James III' (*Studies in Scottish Literature* vol XIV, 1979, pp 123–36).

With fair tretie yit scho gart hir upryse,
And to the burde thay went and togidder sat,
And scantlie had thay drunkin anis or twyse,
Quhen in come Gib Hunter, our jolie Cat,
And bad God speid; the burges up with that,
And till her hole scho went as fire on flint;
Bawdronis the uther be the bak hes hint.

Fra fute to fute he kest hir to and fra,
Quhylis up, quhylis doun, als cant as ony kid;
Quhylis wald he lat hir rin under the stra,
Quhylis wald he wink, and play with hir buk heid.
Thus to the selie mous grit pane he did,
Quhill at the last, throw fortune and gude hap,
Betwix ane burde and the wall scho crap.

Syne up in haist behind ane parraling
Scho clam so hie, that Gilbert micht not get hir,
And be the clukis craftelie can hing,
Till he wes gane; hir cheir wes all the better.
Syne doun scho lap quhen thair wes nane to let hir,
And to the burges mous loud can scho cry,
'Fairweill, sister, thy feist heir I defy!

Thy mangerie is mingit all with cair,
Thy guse is gude, thy gansell sour as gall.
The subcharge off they service is bot sair;
Sa sall thow find heir efterwart na fall.
I thank yone curtyne and yone perpall wall
Of my defence now fra yone crewell beist.
Almichtie God, keip me fra sic ane feist!'

ROBERT HENRYSON (*c.* 1420–*c.* 1490)
from *The Taill of the Uponlandis Mous, and the Burges Mous*

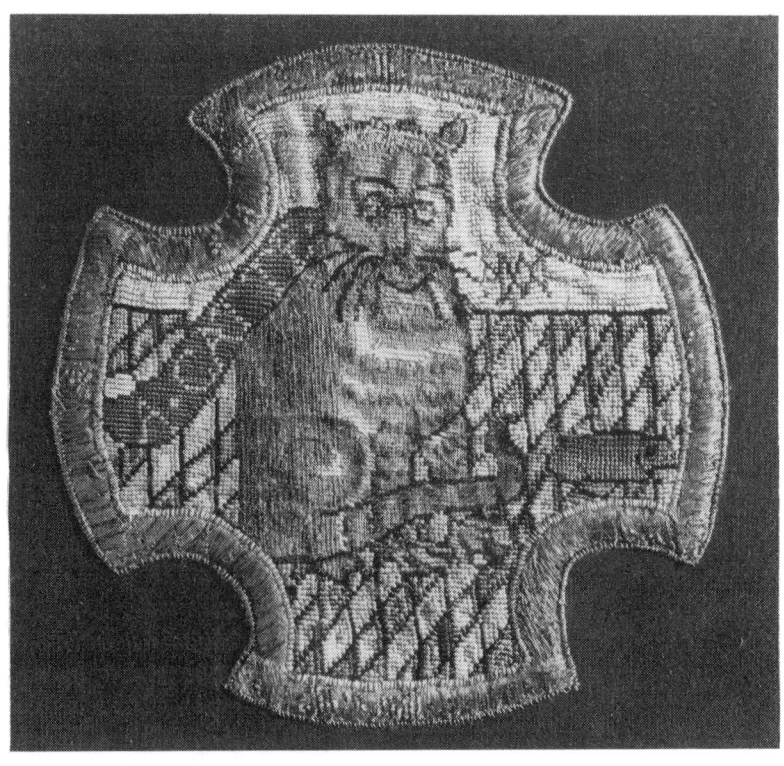

THE CAMERONIAN CAT

The Cameronians were followers of Richard Cameron, a Scottish Covenanter, who rejected the indulgence granted to nonconforming ministers and formally renounced allegiance to Charles II; they became the Reformed Presbyterian Church of Scotland. Cameron was executed in 1680.

There was a Ca - me - ro - nian cat Was
hunt - ing for a prey, And in the house she
catch'd a mouse, Up - on the Sab - bath day.

The Whig, being offended
    At such an act profane,
Laid by his book, the cat he took,
    And bound her in a chain.

'Thou damn'd, thou cursed creature,
    This deed so dark with thee,
Think'st thou to bring to hell below,
    My holy wife and me?

Assure thyself, that for the deed
    Thou blood for blood shalt pay,
For killing of the Lord's own mouse
    Upon the Sabbath-day.'

The presbyter laid by the book,
   And earnestly he pray'd,
That the great sin the cat had done
   Might not on him be laid.

And straight to execution
   Poor baudrons she was drawn,
And high hang'd up upon a tree;
   Mess John he sung a psalm.

And when the work was ended,
   They thought the cat near dead;
She gave a paw, and then a mew,
   And stretched out her head.

'Thy name,' said he, 'shall certainly
   A beacon still remain,
A terror unto evil ones,
   For evermore. Amen.'

The Jacobite Relics of Scotland,
ed JAMES HOGG, 1819

THE CATTIE SITS IN THE KILN-RING SPINNING

The cattie sits in the kiln-ring,
    Spinning, spinning;
And by came a little wee mousie,
    Rinning, rinning.

'Oh what's that you're spinning, my loesome,
    Loesome lady?'
'I'm spinning a sark to my young son,'
    Said she, said she.

'Weel mot he brook it, my loesome,
    Loesome lady.'
'Gif he dinna brook it weel, he may brook it ill,'
    Said she, said she.

'I soopit my house, my loesome,
    Loesome lady.'
''Twas a sign ye didna sit amang dirt then,'
    Said she, said she.

'I fand twall pennies, my winsome,
    Winsome lady.'
''Twas a sign ye warna sillerless,'
    Said she, said she.

'I gaed to the market, my loesome,
    Loesome lady.'
''Twas a sign ye didna sit at hame then,'
    Said she, said she.

'I coft a sheepie's head, my winsome,
    Winsome lady.'
''Twas a sign ye warna kitchenless,'
    Said she, said she.

'I put it in my pottie to boil, my loesome,
　　Loesome lady.'
"Twas a sign ye didna eat it raw,'
　　Said she, said she.

'I put it in my winnock to cool, my winsome,
　　Winsome lady.'
"Twas a sign ye didna burn your chafts then,'
　　Said she, said she.

'By came a cattie, and ate it a' up, my loesome,
　　Loesome lady.'
'And sae will I you — worrie, worrie — guash, guash,'
　　Said she, said she.

ROBERT CHAMBERS,
Popular Rhymes of Scotland

Horse in stable with cat stalking rats. James Howe

ON A CAT, AGEING

He blinks upon the hearth-rug,
And yawns in deep content,
Accepting all the comforts
That Providence has sent.

Louder he purrs, and louder,
In one glad hymn of praise
For all the night's adventures,
For quiet, restful days.

Life will go on for ever,
With all that cat can wish:
Warmth and the glad procession
Of fish and milk and fish.

Only — the thought disturbs him —
He's noticed once or twice,
The times are somehow breeding
A nimbler race of mice.

ALEXANDER GRAY (1882–1968)

LITERARY CATS

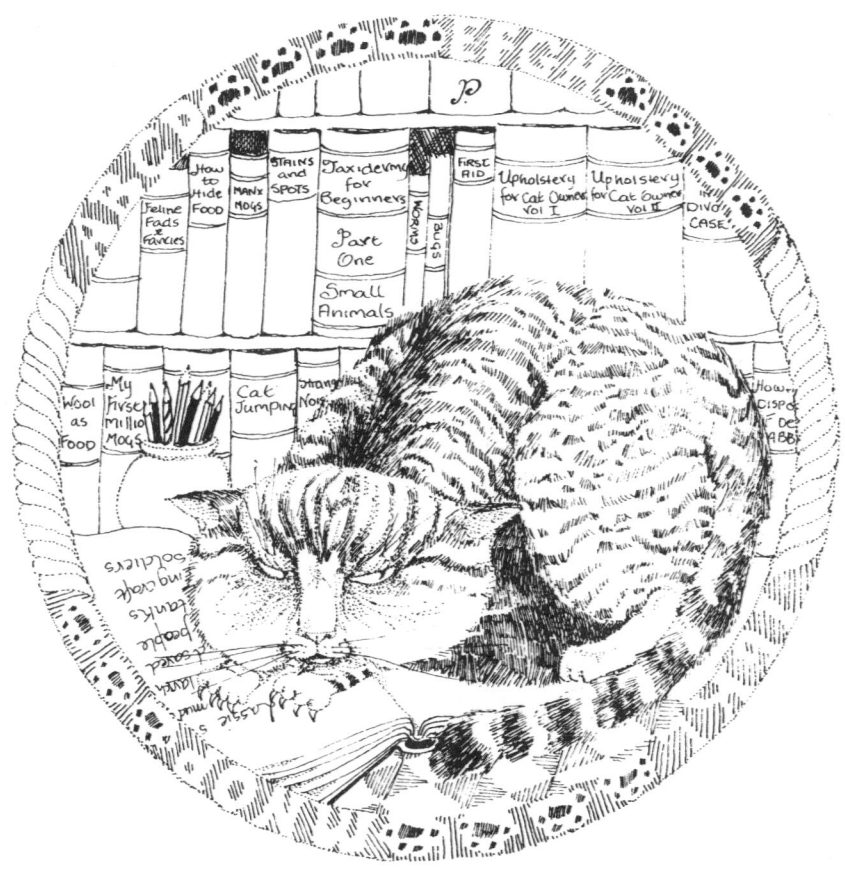

'An excellent companion for
A literary gentleman, a cat',
said fat auld Gautier,
And, Dod, he was richt, at that.
                    SYDNEY GOODSIR SMITH

Of course, cats are not the only animal companions chosen by literary folk (merely the ideal): Scott loved his hounds more, especially Nimrod, and is to be considered something of an opsimath where cats are concerned; and cats formed only part of the menagerie maintained at Ravenna by Byron ('half a Scot by birth, and bred a whole one', *Don Juan*, X.xvii) as his journal demonstrates: 'Fed the two cats, the hawk, and the tame (but not *tamed*) crow' (5 January 1821); 'The falcon pretty brisk — the cats large and noisy — the monkeys I have not looked to since the cold weather, as they suffer by being brought up' (6 January 1821). Nevertheless, the number of writers who have either owned cats or written about them is a very large one and includes Victor Hugo, Alexandre Dumas, Baudelaire, Colette, Keats, Thomas Gray, Wordsworth, Thomas Hardy, W B Yeats, Mark Twain, and Edgar Allan Poe as well as a strong Scottish contingent.

SIR WALTER SCOTT, HINSE AND OTHERS

'The greatest advance of age which I have yet found is liking a *cat* an animal I detested . . .' (Letter to Lord Montagu, 1822) Scott's favourite was 'Mr Hinse the brindled cat', acquired about 1812. This cat, described by J G Lockhart as 'a venerable tom-cat, fat and sleek', was named Hinse of Hinsfeldt from a common name in the German folk tales Scott translated for his children.

Scott loved his animals but was not sentimental: 'My cat has eat two or three birds while regaling on the crumbs that were thrown for them — this was a breach of hospitality — but *oportet vivare*' he wrote to the Duke of Buccleuch in 1816. About this time he added 'a most romantic inmate' to his family,

> a large bloodhound allow'd to be the finest dog of the kind in Scotland perfectly gentle affectionate and good-natured and the darling of all the children. . . . He is between the deer greyhound and mastiff with a shaggy mane like a lion and always sits beside me at dinner — his head as high as the back of my chair. Yet it will gratify you to know that a favourite cat keeps him in the greatest possible order insists upon all rights of precedence and scratches with impunity the nose of an animal who would make no bones of a wolf and pulls down a red-deer without fear or difficulty. I heard my friend set up some most piteous howls and I assure you the noise was no joke — all occasioned by his fear of passing puss who had stationed himself on the stairs. (To John Richardson, 1816)

This feline dominance is confirmed in the American writer Washington Irving's account of a visit to Abbotsford:

> Among the other important and privileged members of the household who figured in attendance at dinner was a large grey cat, who, I observed, was regaled from time to time with tit-bits from the table. This sage grimalkin was a favourite of both master and mistress, and slept at night in their room, and Scott laughingly observed, that one of the least wise parts of their establishment was, that the window was left open at night for puss to go in and out. The cat assumed a kind of ascendancy among the quadrupeds — sitting in state in Scott's armchair, and occasionally stationing himself on a chair beside the door, as if to review his subjects as they passed, giving each dog a cuff beside the ears as he went by. This clapper-clawing was always taken in good part; it appeared to be, in fact, a mere act of sovereignty on the

Sir Walter Scott with his bloodhound and his cat Hinse. Sir John Watson Gordon

part of grimalkin, to remind the others of their vassalage; which they acknowledged by the most perfect acquiescence. A general harmony prevailed between sovereign and subjects, and they would all sleep together in the sunshine. (*Abbotsford and Newstead Abbey*, 1850)

An anecdote told by Mr Adolphus, recounted in J G Lockhart's life of Scott, reveals that Sir Walter's dogs, and in particular, his favourite Nimrod,

though very docile and unobtrusive animals in the house, were sometimes a little wild in their frolics out of doors. One day when I was walking with Sir Walter and Miss Scott, we passed a cottage, at the door of which sat on one side a child, and on the other a slumbering cat. Nimrod bounded from us in great gaiety, and the unsuspecting cat had scarcely time to squall before she was demolished. The poor child set up a dismal wail. Miss Scott was naturally distressed, and Sir Walter a good deal out of countenance. However, he put an end to the subject by saying, with an assumed stubbornness, 'Well! the cat is worried;' but his purse was in his hand; Miss Scott was despatched to the house, and I am very sure it was not his fault if the cat had a poor funeral. In the confusion of the moment, I am afraid the culprit went off without even a reprimand. (*Memoirs of the Life of Sir Walter Scott*, 2nd edn, 1839)

Hinse finally met his match in Nimrod. In April 1827, writing to his son Charles, Scott described the cat's death: 'The young bloodhound Nimrod has dispatched poor old Hinzie the stoutness of whose heart led him always to attack the mighty huntsman before the Lord till at last he paid the kain as we say.' In another letter written the same day, to his son Walter's wife, he wrote, 'I must say Hinzie had been the aggressor in former encounters but I was vexed to lose my old friend.' He did not forget Hinse easily: in December of the following year he was writing to his friend John Richardson,

... I (trusting there can be no bad consequences) was rather amused with Mrs [Joanna] Baillie's cat who worried the dog. It is just like her Mrs who beats the male race of authors out of the pitt in describing the higher passions that are more proper to their sex than hers. Alack a day my poor cat Hinze my acquaintance and in some sort my friend of fifteen years was snapd at once by the paynim Nimrod. What could I say to him but what Brantome said to some *fouiller* [?ferrailleur] who had been too successful in a duel 'Ah mon grand ami vous avez tué mon autre grand ami.' It is a good thing to have read queer books they always furnish you with a parallel case in your afflictions.

Cat at Abbotsford (possibly Sir Walter Scott's Cat Hinse).
Attrib. David Ramsay Hay

Study. *Northern Looking Glass* (1825)

A NEFARIOUS CAT

John Galt wrote his own deathbed scene in his *Autobiography*, describing his death as 'something like a cat that I was at the drowning of in my boyish years: a country carter, who looked over my shoulder at the sight, on seeing the poor animal, remarked on the catastrophe, that it would "take pains to kill her" '. Another cat he never forgot was the one he met on the Greenock road:

I remember very distinctly the occasion on which I was first sensible of the influence of the Muses, though I do not recollect the exact date. It was in 1785 or 86, when about six years old, during one of those annual migratory transits from Irvine to Greenock, alluded to in the early part of my Autobiography.

I had received two young larks, on leaving Irvine, to take with me to Greenock, and on the road, I suppose, caught from them some tuneful infection, for I was induced to begin a kind of ballad in celebration of their birth, parentage, and intended education. Nothing of the poetry can now be rescued from oblivion, but the birds were carried to Greenock; one of them, however, was soon after crushed to death beneath my heel, in consequence of a nefarious cat attempting to kidnap his brother with the zest and zeal of an Edinburgh critic seizing a poetling. In the endeavour to defend the one minor, the other fell from my hand, and while in the act of inflicting summary vengeance on the unprincipled aggressor, I trode the helpless victim as flat as a pancake. The remembrance of the accident makes my heart bleed even unto this day.

JOHN GALT,
The Literary Life of John Galt, 1833

Dead game. John Kay

THOMAS AND JANE CARLYLE:
CATS AND DOGS

Thomas liked cats but rarely wrote about them; while Jane regarded them as a necessary nuisance — tolerated for T.C.'s sake and for their usefulness in keeping down rats and mice. She found them a disturbing influence in her household — her own tastes were for lapdogs and canaries — and frequently complained in her correspondence of the various cats who at one time or another shared the house at Number 5 Cheyne Row.

Nero, Jane's favourite dog, arrived at Cheyne Row in 1849 and soon made friends with the black female cat already there. Carlyle wrote, 'Directly on the dining-room door opening' Nero and the cat 'used to come waltzing in . . . in the height of joy, like Harlequin and Columbine, as I once heard remarked and did not forget.' The cat was henceforth known as Columbine — the only Carlyle cat ever to be given a name.

The following year, while Carlyle was staying with friends in Hampshire he received this letter:

Dear Master

I take the liberty to write to you myself (my mistress being out of the way of writing to you she says) that you may know Columbine and I are quite well, and play about as usual. There was no dinner yesterday to speak of; I had for my share only a piece of biscuit that might have been round the world; and if Columbine got anything at all, I didn't see it. . . . I wasn't taken to walk on account of its being wet. And nobody came, but a man for 'burial rate'; and my mistress gave him a rowing because she wasn't going to be buried here at all. Columbine and I don't mind where we are buried . . . no more at present from your
        Obedient little dog,
        Nero.

Nero was not so well-disposed towards the white cat who succeeded Columbine. In a letter to Carlyle in 1852 Jane wrote:

Going down into the kitchen the morning after my return from Sherborne, I spoke to the white cat, in common politeness, and even stroked her; whereupon the jealousy of Nero rose to a pitch. He snapped and barked at me, then flew at the cat quite savage.

In 1860, of the then current cat, Jane wrote:

For several days there had been *that* in her eyes when raised to my
canary, which filled my heart with alarm. I sent express for a
carpenter, and had the cage attached to the drawing-room ceiling, with
an elaborate apparatus of chain and pulley and weight. . . . And there it
had swung for two days, to Mr C's intense disgust, who regards this
pet as '*the most inanely chimerical of all*' — the cat meanwhile spending
all its spare time in gazing up at the bird with eyes aflame! But it was
safe *now*, I thought! and went out for a walk. On my return Charlotte
[the housemaid] met me with 'Oh! Whatever *do* you think the cat has
gone and done?' 'Eaten my canary?' — 'No, *far worse!* — pulled down
the cage and the weight, and broke the chain and upset the little table
and broken everything on it!' — 'And not eaten the canary?' — 'Oh, I
suppose the dreadful crash she made frightened *herself*; for I met *her*
running downstairs as I ran up — tho' the cage was on the floor, and
the door open and the canary in such a way!'

In 1865 she wrote to her housemaid Jessie about the same cat:

I still hope he [T.C.] may not come till I myself am home first! But —
if he should — there is one thing you must attend to, and which you
would not think of without being told! — that cat!! — I wish she were
dead! But I can't shorten her days! because — you see — my poor wee
dog liked her! Well! there she is — and as long as she attends Mr C at
his meals (she doesn't care a snuff of tobacco for him at any other
times!) so long will Mr C continue to give her bits of meat, and
dribbles of milk, to the ruination of carpets and hearth-rugs! — I have
over and over again pointed out to him the stains she has made — but
he won't believe them her doing! — And the diningroom carpet was so
old and ugly, that it wasn't worth rows with one's Husband about!
Now, however, that nice new cloth must be protected against the Cat-
abuse. So what I wish is that you would shut up the creature when Mr
C has breakfast, or dinner, or tea. And if he remarks on her absence,
say it was my express desire. He has no idea what a selfish, immoral,
improper beast she is, nor what mischief she does to the carpets.

Finally, a glimpse of Carlyle in old age from a letter written in 1874 by his
niece Mary Aitken:

We have got a nice large fat cat here. Mr Carlyle likes it so much. He
takes the hearth brush every morning and smoothes down its fur; puss
likes it exceedingly and stretches herself out when she sees him
coming; she shuts her eyes and pretends to be asleep.

Thomas Carlyle and Cat

Black cat on mantelpiece. Oscar Marzaroli, Exhibition of Cat Paintings, Mayfest 1987

CONCERNING CATS

Best known as historian, anthropologist, editor of the 'colour' Fairy Books, poet, translator, and solver of historical mysteries, Andrew Lang was also a prolific journalist, book reviewer — and cat lover. This is a selection of pieces from his column 'At the Sign of the Ship' which he wrote for *Longman's Magazine* in 1898.

'Thus freely speaketh Montaigne concerning cats,' says Izaak Walton, who plainly disapproved of such liberties. They are increasing; and I observe authors who speak concerning cats with a familiarity and a levity most distasteful. Mr W L Alden, for instance, is reported to boast that he is 'an honorary cat,' much as if a man were to call himself an honorary member of the Roxburghe Club. In dealing with cats, this author permits himself great and disrespectful license. Mr Louis Robinson, also, in what he says about cats (in 'Wild Traits in Tame Animals'), treats cats as if they were subject to the ordinary laws of evolution, as understood by popular science. These laws, at least in books and papers of popular science, seem to me a set of fairy tales. Mr Mivart, devoting a whole volume to the cat, probably handles with respect an animal which was a kind of god long, long before the days of Moses. But my present contest is with Mr Robinson.

What does this agreeable author really know, on sound documentary evidence, about the history of the domestic puss? He begins with its prehistoric period, which he fancifully constructs out of the habits of the tame animal. Now these habits vary in different cats. Thus a regretted friend of my own, a black cat with a great deal of *retenue*, never went near another cat's dish; while, if another cat approached *his* dish, he instantly retired. 'Mere food,' he seemed to say, 'is not worth a wrangle.' He withdrew from all forms of competition, like a dignified Royal cat in exile. On the other hand, many cats, and one of mine in particular, always desert their own platter (however tempting) for that of their neighbour. Which of these opposite traits is primitive? 'In its natural state,' says Mr Robinson, 'the cat is not in the habit of associating with greedy companions.' But, if you give a cat the leg of a grouse, partridge, or other game bird, he does show signs of greed and ferocity, growling as he feeds. Therefore in his natural state, when he caught game birds, I conceive that the cat *did* associate with greedy companions, and growled to keep them away, just as newspapers growl at foreign nations. How did cats acquire their taste for fish? Has any one seen a wild cat angling?

That cats originally lived in forests is very likely. The wild cat, Mr Robinson urges, is not nomadic, does not gad about, but has a settled home. Now this, perhaps, explains why very low nomadic races, like the Australians, have not domesticated cats, though they have tamed the dingo, or wild dog. The cat would go home when the restless human tribe broke up its camp — the dog, on the other hand, likes change of scenery. The cat's homing instinct is notorious. I have known a cat taken from St Andrews to Perth. He came back in less than a week. Did he swim the Tay and Eden, or did he travel by rail, changing at Dundee and Leuchars? In either case he showed great sagacity, accompanied by love of home. These qualities, I think, have prevented nomadic peoples from taming the cat. He declines to wander with them.

Mr Robinson thinks that the tailless Manx Cat 'is probably a representative of some ancient wild species.' But I long ago accounted for the Manx cat's want of a tail on principles of evolution. Man is a Celtic island. The Celts (in Brittany, at least) believe that if you tread on a cat's tail a serpent will come out and bite you. This made people shy of cats with tails. But a tailless cat, being born by a pure fluke (see Darwin on Sports) and transmitting the peculiarity to its offspring, these cats with no tails were especially adapted to their Celtic environment. People could make pets of *them*, without fear of serpents. The other cats were killed out, or died for lack of friendly treatment. This could only occur in insular conditions: hence the Isle of Man possesses Manx cats. But why the Isle of Mull does not, I do not know, unless the superstition about treading on cat's tails is Brythonic, or Welsh, not Gaelic.

Concerning cats, Mr Walter Pollock tells me that catasthma is a recognised malady, like hay-fever, and that people may acquire it from the contiguity of cats, even when cats are not known, through any normal channel of sense, to be present. One often knows when a *dog* is in the room, or has been there, without deriving information from the eyes or ears. Mr Pollock adds the story of a percipient who is 'devoted to all kinds of beasts and birds, including *cats*, by will. But she cannot gratify that will as to cats. She called on me one day in London. I knew of her peculiarity in this way, and, expecting her call, had turned the cats out. She had not been ten minutes in the room when she showed every symptom, very marked, of "hay-fever" — streaming eyes, violent sneezing, *tout le tremblement*. I took it for hay-fever and offered remedies, but she said, "I'm very sorry, for you know I love all animals; but I'm sure there's a cat in the room." There was one, that had slunk back and hidden itself under the sofa where she was sitting.'

This is proof of *catasthma*, but what one wants proof of is *an undefined horror* caused by the presence, not normally known, of a cat in the room.

ANDREW LANG (1844–1912)

HECTOR HUGH MUNRO AND CATS

'To me,' wrote Ethel Munro of her brother Hector Hugh Munro, 'his strongest characteristics were — whimsicality, keen sense of humour, love of animals, and pride in being Highland.' He loved cats particularly: in his childhood, living under a tyranny of aunts, he and his brother and sister 'had charming cats, who gave us all the affection the grown-ups did not know how to show.' And for the rest of his life cats were always prominent among the animals that seemed to gather round him wherever he went. While in Burma, as an officer in the Military Police, he even kept a tiger kitten:

> we have great games together. It has not learnt how to drink properly yet and immerses its nose in the milk, then it gets mad with the saucer and shakes it, which sends the milk all over its paws, upon which it swears horribly. . . . The kitten throws off the cat and assumes the tiger when it is fed; I have to throw its food (generally the head of a chicken) and then bolt; it is making the day hideous with its growling now, as I gave it the head and wing, and it is trying to eat both at once.

Eight years later (in 1901) he describes the effect of his Aunt Tom on Edinburgh thus:

> we spent a happy hour driving from one hostelry to another in search of rooms, Aunt Tom reiterating the existence of a Writer to the Signet who went away and let his room 30 years ago, and ought to be doing it still. 'Anyhow,' she said, 'we are seeing Edinburgh,' much as Moses might have informed the companions of his 40 years' wanderings that they were seeing Asia. Then we came here, and she took rooms after scolding the manageress, servants and entire establishment nearly out of their senses because everything was not to her liking. I hurriedly explained to everybody that my aunt was tired and upset after a long journey, and disappointed at not getting the rooms she had expected; after I had comforted two chambermaids and the boots, who were crying quietly in corners, and coaxed the hotel kitten out of the waste-paper basket, I went to get a shave and a wash.

And a limerick from a letter to his sister:

> There once was a Grand Duke of Baden
> Said 'The Things that go on in My Garden!
> I really can't stand;
> Not a Cat in the Land
> But gives itself Heirs in my Garden.'

THE ACHIEVEMENT OF THE CAT

In the political history of nations it is no uncommon experience to find
States and peoples which but a short time since were in bitter conflict
and animosity with each other, settled down comfortably on terms of
mutual goodwill and even alliance. The natural history of the social
developments of species affords a similar instance in the coming-
together of two once warring elements, now represented by civilized
man and the domestic cat. The fiercely waged struggle which went on
between humans and felines in those far-off days when sabre-toothed
tiger and cave lion contended with primeval man, has long ago been
decided in favour of the most fitly equipped combatant — the Thing
with a Thumb — and the descendants of the dispossessed family are
relegated today, for the most part, to the waste lands of jungle and
veld, where an existence of self-effacement is the only alternative to
extermination. But the *felis catus*, or whatever species was the ancestor
of the modern domestic cat (a vexed question at present), by a master-
stroke of adaptation avoided the ruin of its race, and 'captured' a place
in the very keystone of the conqueror's organization. For not as a
bond-servant or dependent has this proudest of mammals entered the
human fraternity; not as a slave like the beasts of burden, or a humble
camp-follower like the dog. The cat is domestic only as far as suits its
own ends; it will not be kennelled or harnessed nor suffer any dictation
as to its goings out or comings in. Long contact with the human race
has developed in it the art of diplomacy, and no Roman Cardinal of
mediaeval days knew better how to ingratiate himself with his
surroundings than a cat with a saucer of cream on its mental horizon.
But the social smoothness, the purring innocence, the softness of the
velvet paw may be laid aside at a moment's notice, and the sinuous
feline may disappear, in deliberate aloofness, to a world of roofs and
chimney-stacks, where the human element is distanced and dis-
regarded. Or the innate savage spirit that helped its survival in the
bygone days of tooth and claw may be summoned forth from beneath
the sleek exterior, and the torture-instinct (common alone to human
and feline) may find free play in the death-throes of some luckless bird
or rodent. It is, indeed, no small triumph to have combined the
untrammelled liberty of primeval savagery with the luxury which only
a highly developed civilization can command; to be lapped in the soft
stuffs that commerce has gathered from the far ends of the world; to
bask in the warmth that labour and industry have dragged from the
bowels of the earth; to banquet on the dainties that wealth has

bespoken for its table, and withal to be a free son of nature, a mighty hunter, a spiller of life-blood. This is the victory of the cat. But besides the credit of success the cat has other qualities which compel recognition. The animal which the Egyptians worshipped as divine, which the Romans venerated as a symbol of liberty, which Europeans in the ignorant Middle Ages anathematized as an agent of demonology, has displayed to all ages two closely blended characteristics — courage and self-respect. No matter how unfavourable the circumstances, both qualities are always to the fore. Confront a child, a puppy, and a kitten with a sudden danger; the child will turn instinctively for assistance, the puppy will grovel in abject submission to the impending visitation, the kitten will brace its tiny body for a frantic resistance. And disassociate the luxury-loving cat from the atmosphere of social comfort in which it usually contrives to move, and observe it critically under the adverse conditions of civilization — that civilization which can impel a man to the degradation of clothing himself in tawdry ribald garments and capering mountebank dances in the streets for the earning of the few coins that keep him on the respectable, or non-criminal, side of society. The cat of the slums and

Smudge the People's Palace cat

alleys, starved, outcast, harried, still keeps amid the prowlings of its adversity the bold, free, panther-tread with which it paced of yore the temple courts of Thebes, still displays the self-reliant watchfulness which man has never taught it to lay aside. And when its shifts and clever managings have not sufficed to stave off inexorable fate, when its enemies have proved too strong or too many for its defensive powers, it dies fighting to the last, quivering with the choking rage of mastered resistance, and voicing in its death-yell that agony of bitter remonstrance which human animals, too, have flung at the powers that may be; the last protest against a destiny that might have made them happy — and has not.

HECTOR HUGO MUNRO (SAKI) (1870–1916)
The Square Egg, 1924

GRIGI, RUM AND EIGG

In 1931 I was elected Rector of Glasgow University and at the beginning of my second year of office after the publication of my third volume of war memoirs I was prosecuted under the Official Secrets Act. This was a bad financial setback, for although the fine was a mere £100 the book was suppressed and what with one thing and another this farcical prosecution cost me nearly £5,000.

This made it imperative for me to start working again as hard as in the earlier days of Jethou, and I went to live in a cottage on Barra in the Outer Hebrides, having fallen in love with the island when I had visited it first five years earlier and returned there several times. I gave up living in Eilean Aigas but left behind Nellie Boyte in the gardener's cottage to look after the cats.

In the cottage was a small grey tabby, called Grigi. She had been just a cat about the place until Christina MacSween, my other secretary, and I came to the cottage and it was remarkable how quickly she responded to intelligent conversation.

During the last twenty years the cat has recovered the esteem in which it was held until the Victorian spirit made an idol of the dog. It is significant that the dog has provided no great stories like Dick Whittington and his Cat or Puss in Boots. In the Nursery Rhymes, too, the cat always has precedence.

'Pussy cat, pussy cat, where have you been?
I've been to London to see the Queen.'

An idea grew up that cats preferred places to people, and those who could win the easy flattery of a dog were baffled by the failure of most cats to respond immediately to patronage.

'Cats are so selfish. Cats think only of their own comfort. Cats are not affectionate. Cats are so cruel. Cats are such thieves . . .' And on it goes: the comment of the empty human mind that can only think in banalities oft heard and oft repeated.

Siamese cats were regarded as exceptions and praised because they had canine qualities. The only dogs whose qualities they share are Chows and Pekinese and that is because Chows and Pekinese have feline qualities. At last more and more people are realizing that many of the qualities they admire in Siamese exist in ordinary cats if they take the trouble to bring out those qualities. But they must win the cat's respect and love; they must not wait for the cat to make the first approach, because if they do nine times out of ten they will wait in vain. I can call a noctambulant cat on the other side of a London street

Caricature of Compton Mackenzie – A Modern Monastic. 'Scoticus' (1936)

and it will cross over to have a brief colloquy with me, but those able to do this are in a small minority.

Grigi, that small grey tabby, astonished Ruairidh Dubh (dark Roderick), the owner of the cottage, by her response to the novel attention paid to her. Then finding that if he paid her attention she would presently respond to his advances Ruairidh became immensely proud of Grigi and would boast about her intelligence at the least excuse. He started talking to her in Gaelic and declared she followed what he was saying better in Gaelic than in English. He was proud too of the way Grigi would go fishing in the burn and hook the small fish out with her paw. Then one day she hooked an eel and Ruairidh was prouder of her than ever.

That summer Grigi produced two kittens, one a tabby, the other a tortoiseshell. We called them Rum and Eigg. They were born in the small sitting-room in which I worked almost incessantly for fifteen months, and once again delight in the company of a cat and of kittens growing into cats sustained my spirit. In due course Eigg was given to an old crofter who lived alone and felt that Eigg was the companion he needed. With him she lived happily and was a comfort to his loneliness.

In the following year I was asked to lecture in Buenos Aires, Montevideo and Rio de Janeiro, and Christina MacSween took Rum to live with her mother in Tarbert in the island of Harris before she joined my wife and myself to make the trip to South America. Rum became devoted to Mrs MacSween who used to feed her with raw eggs and cream, a dish Rum loved. Every Sunday she would walk to church with Mrs MacSween and when she saw across the loch the congregation coming out she would walk round to meet her on her way home.

Rum had one taste in food which within my experience is unique. She had what amounted to a passion for melons. She would growl more loudly over a slice of melon than a captured mouse, and she would not leave a fragment of the rind. She had developed this taste as a kitten and kept it to the end of her days when like so many much loved cats and dogs she was killed by a wretched car. Eigg could never understand her sister's taste for melon. She used to sit and gaze in perplexity at Rum growling over her slice. Once she tried a bit of melon herself and shuddered with disgust. I have known a dog who liked grapes and gooseberries: he used to gather the latter from bushes himself. My thrush liked treacle, but I have never known a cat or dog or bird who liked melons. I tried Rum with other fruit, but without success.

COMPTON MACKENZIE (1883–1972),
Cats' Company, 1960

John Kay and Cat, drawn and engraved by himself (1786)

WILLIAM SOUTAR'S DREAM

The poet William Soutar (1898–1943) as well as keeping detailed diaries regularly recorded his dreams. Here is one of his cat dreams, entered on 23 February 1923:

> Had some sport with a cat-tiger. I remember it was just the size of an ordinary cat, first of all. It leapt into my arms and I began to play with it. I believe it scratched me. Later I found myself struggling with a huge animal, half-cat, half-tiger. It had a chain half way down its throat and I was pulling with all my strength — just like a fisherman with some great fish. At the back of my mind was the idea that this cat-tiger was to be yoked to some sort of vehicle. Suddenly I was struck with the not-extraordinary idea that kindness might win over the beast; so I gave the giant-cat a few gentle pats on the head. In a moment it was purring around me, and my dream faded away amid general good-humouredness.

He added in the margin: 'The strength of kindness and the futility of strength.'

from *Diaries of a Dying Man*, ed A. SCOTT

STORMY DAY AND A CAT, NOVEMBER

The gods is mairchin owre the roof
With ten-ton buits on their feet —
Valhalla houls in the lum,
Trees snap, their branches hurl
Across this high windae here . . . and
The haill world teems in a second Deluge.

I sit idle as my cat
Immobile, gazes at the interesting scene,
Intent in seeming wonder.

      ('An excellent companion for
      A literary gentleman, a cat',
      Said fat auld Gautier,
      And, Dod, he was richt, at that.)

And sae bemusit by the storm outby,
Tak ma pen to scrieve a word t'ye,
Bypittin mair important cares
Wi the full approval o' a furry cat
That maybe kens the message
That I send, my love, sweetmeat, bluid-drap —
Or maybe juist is watchin
The rain dingin doun,
Blawn by gust and squalls
And great drifts o' leaves . . . leaves . . .
A million leaves, impalpable as Paradise
      (As human dreams for us, *mon chat*)
Through the streamin windae in between, *hélas!*
      (And could be richt, at that,
          Mon Théophile, n'est-ce pas?)

Nou the gods on the roof again . . .
Clump . . . clump . . . their ten-ton buits —
          Ah me!
Come on buckle to, *mon vieux*.
Aye weill, I will. *Adieu! Adieu, chérie!*

And pray for Ptah
The Inscrutable
In Holy Egypt.
      Enshallah!

SYDNEY GOODSIR SMITH

POETICAL CATS

(The Northern Muse)

'I'd rather be a kitten and cry, Mew! than write the best poetry in the world'
SIR WALTER SCOTT (letter to Allan Cunningham, 1822)

Certain poets seem particularly attracted to cats: they cry Mew! *and* write
good poetry. The presence in a domestic situation of a mysterious animal,
'tame but not *tamed*' continually exerts a fascination: 'the tiger who eats
from the hand', as the Japanese saying is; and much cat poetry explores this
ambivalence; for example, Maurice Lindsay's 'Certain Killers' and Alastair
Reid's 'Propinquity'. There is also, as Gautier wrote in his introduction to
Baudelaire's *Fleurs du Mal*, a nocturnal side to cats, strange and cabalistic,
which is very seductive to the poet. This aspect is perhaps hinted at in
Joseph Macleod's 'A Strange Cat Got In' or 'Cat-Faith' by Alastair Reid.

George MacBeth's 'Fourteen Ways of Touching the Peter' is the well-
known case history of the human relationship with the cat; George Bruce
and Brian McCabe ponder the meaning of cats at the window; and Edwin
Morgan's group of international concrete cats, including the definitive
Scotch cat, forms a humorous nucleus of this short anthology of poems by
modern Scottish writers.

POETRY CIRCLE IN A SQUARE ROOM

In the centre of the room
a squat man in a bulgy suit
has put his cap under the chair
upside down into which he coils
a snake like a scarf.
He knows it is not a snake.

It might be convenient if it were
for his nostrils sense the
woman enter, seat herself behind
in the far corner. As she crosses
her legs under the red silk
dressing gown there is the
silk worm sound in his ears.

She contemplates the grey,
horn-rimmed girl with flat
shoes (perhaps she can write)
sitting on the outermost edge,
angular in the front row.
She opens a new note-book.

Snow falls. Snow falls.
A black cat is at the window.
The lecturer will not let
the poem in, dismisses
its green eyes to the darkness.
The black cat leaps from snow,
stares at the pane,
silent, asserting nothing:
leap—a felt movement,

effortlessly creating the
moment that is one thing,
her poise, less precarious,
she acknowledges, perhaps,
our world inside. The snow,
a blank page, acknowledges
her delicate tread, her imprint
of a moon-lit traverse.

Precise shadow, you are
a presence to be shut out.
Admitted, your intolerable
completeness would destroy us.

GEORGE BRUCE

CERTAIN KILLERS

You'd think a mouse so mere a thing
it shouldn't be too hard to kill.

Men believe it crumbs germs
from daily swept-under boards;
women shriek up chairs for fear
it runs against their privacies.

I laid a baited trap. By night
The sprung bar pushed eyes
out of the crushed head. By day
blood ran down disposable whiskers.

I could, of course, keep a cat
to eat my scraps of chopped meat;
but I like birds—they keep their distance—
and cats think all cheeps
signal their pounce of destruction.
Besides, I don't think I could stand
being contempt's glared target
for not doing my own small murders.

MAURICE LINDSAY

FOURTEEN WAYS OF TOUCHING THE PETER

I
You can push
your thumb
in the
ridge
between his
shoulder-blades
to please him.

II
Starting
at its root,
you can let
his whole
tail
flow
through your hand.

III
Forming
a fist
you can let
him rub
his bone
skull
against it, hard.

IV
When he makes
bread,
you can lift
him
by his under-
sides on your
knuckles.

V
In hot
weather
you can itch
the fur
under
his chin. He
likes that.

VI
At night
you can hoist
him
out of his bean-stalk,
sleepily
clutching
paper bags.

VII
Pressing
his head against
your cheek,
you can carry
him
in the dark,
safely.

VIII
In late Autumn
you can find
seeds
adhering
to his fur.
There are
plenty.

IX
You can prise
his jaws
open,
helping
any medicine
he won't
abide, go down.

X
You can touch
his
feet, only
if
he is relaxed.
He
doesn't like it.

XI
You can comb
spare thin
fur
from his coat,
so he won't
get
fur-ball.

XII
You can shake
his rigid
chicken-leg leg,
scouring his
hind-quarters
with his Vim
tongue.

XIII
Dumping
hot fish
on his plate, you can
fend
him off,
pushing
and purring.

XIV
You can have
him shrimp
along you,
breathing,
whenever
you want
to compose poems.

GEORGE MACBETH

BLACK CAT IN A MORNING

Black cat, slink longer: flatten through the grass.
The chaffinch scolds you, pebbling you with chinks
Of quartzy sound, where the green lilac banks
White falls of stillness and green shades of peace.

A shape where topaz eyes may climb and find
The fluttering gone, the dust smelling of green,
The green a royal *déshabillé* of the sun
Tossed on a tree and stitched with its own gold.

And chaffinch rattling from another bush
Shakes with his furious ounce a yard of leaves,
Strikes flints together in his soft throat and moves
In out, out in, two white stripes and a blush.

Black cat pours to the ground, is pool, is cat
That walks finicking away, twitching behind
A stretched foot: sits, is carved, upon the ground,
Drubbing soft tomtoms in his silky throat.

He changes all around him to his scale.
Suburban suns are jungle stripes of fire
And all the mornings that there ever were
Make this one mount and mount and overspill.

And in their drenching where time cannot be,
Amiably blinking in ancestral suns
He swallows chaffinches in stretching yawns
And holds the world down under one soft paw.

NORMAN MACCAIG

THE CAT

Looking up from what I'm doing
(looking up a word, to find out
if it means what I *want* it to . . .)
I find out it's me who's been
looked up—by the unexpected:
outside my window, looking in
is a fat, striped Amazement.
I see myself as I'm seen
by this startled incarnation:
in his eyes' mad, golden moons
there's terror—and recognition.
And I see what I mean to him
whether I want to or not:
man, in his undergrowth of words,
hunting a wild connotation . . .
As I close the curtains on him,
he turns on his tail's questionmark
and leaps into a starless dark
night full of desperate definitions.

BRIAN MCCABE

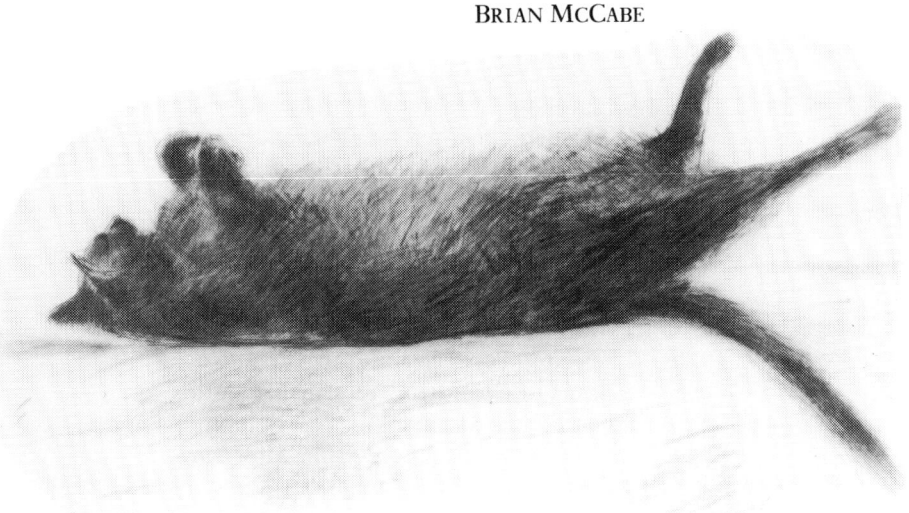

A STRANGE CAT GOT IN

When we arrived home, the wooden cherub on
　　the mantelpiece had fallen and broken a
　　leg. Our cat would not have done that.
　　There was a tumbler chopped in two. Nor
　　that either. In the kitchen the bucket
　　had bent sideways, and the bathroom wash-
　　basin was choked with fragments of scent.
　　Nor that; nor that; nor that. A strange
　　cat had got in.
What's the matter with the boy these days?
　　He used to sunfire his mouth, ever, from
　　his potting and cotted days. Would chatter
　　what he did or required to do. Would rest
　　his head on my knee like a falling star.
　　But now he sits glooming along vacuity:
　　and if he seldom looks, he sees often out-
　　side the house. A strange cat got in.
They do not build houses now, nor motorcars,
　　nor shape shoes, as was. There is always
　　noise of much moving, in day streets and
　　night rooms. We can hardly think any more:
　　it is all processed for us. Even Charity
　　is superannuated by the State. We can barely
　　give to the other poor. A strange cat got in.
We remember the early run up to midnight,
　　scramblings over roofs, secrecies next day.
　　We remember when we raced and were naturesome.
　　Something must have been loose in us,
　　something open to abscess, and a strange
　　cat got in. We have to lock our souls up
　　now before we go to bed, and to insure
　　our tickets of tomorrow morning.
Once, thinking I had trapped the intruder,
　　I hesitated between watering-can and
　　walking-stick. When I returned from this
　　indecision, it was my wife's black jumper,
　　slipped from the supper-table. How long
　　has my wife liked to wear black? How
　　long has she stopped redding up the house
　　when there was no more rush to bed?

We never knew how much more we could live.
    Wars took the cement out of our new
    foundations, and tangled the wires of our
    extensions, how many years ago? Now it
    is idle to dream when there is no more
    time for hope: but there is eagerness to
    dream. Only to dream. And our dreams
    have to go backward.
Did a strange cat get in? Maybe it did.
    But to you it was a friend and usual cat.

JOSEPH GORDON MACLEOD (b. 1903)

FROM THE VIDEO BOX: 15

I know you won't mind if I use your box
for a *cri de coeur*. My, cat, has, gone,
vanished without a trace, I have not seen him
for a week, and I am *quite distracted*.
He is a marmalade cat called Robertson,
he is big and beautiful and an absolute *bumper*
of a creature, you could not miss him,
he is *sui generis* and *sine qua non*.
There *is* a tiny tiny tiny nick
in his left ear which I would *not* mention
but for the identification; he is *all cat*.
And he should be wearing a
smart smooth polished dark brown real leather collar
which was *so* carefully chosen
to go with that *lovely* lovely fluffy warm gold fur,
and his name and address are on it.
To those who are watching—I don't say he's been *abducted*,
it's just he has such a trusting trusting nature,
he would go with anyone for a kind word,
or a *little* fillet sole, he does not *gobble* or snatch,
and he purrs at your legs like a *percolator*.
Well what more can I say,
Robertson is a treasure, a dear, a *rara avis*, a gift—

and if any of you have him I want him back *pronto*.

EDWIN MORGAN

SCOTCH CAT

chee
chee
cheetikiepu
ssiecheetik
iepussieche
etikiepussi
echeetikiep
ussiecheeti
kiepussiech
eetikiepuss
iecheetikie
pussiecheet
ikiepussiec
heeetikiepus
siecheetiki
epussiechee
chee
chee

EDWIN MORGAN

LIKE, LITTLE RUSSIAN CAT

KAKKOTE
HOKKAKK
OTEHOKK
AKKOTEH
OKKAKKO
TEHOKKA
KKOTEHO
KKAKKOT
EHOKKAK
KOTEHOK

EDWIN MORGAN

FRENCH PERSIAN CATS HAVING A BALL

chat
shah   shah
        chat
            chat   shah   cha ha
            shah   chat   cha ha
    shah
    chat
cha
cha

                     ha
                   chat
                   chat
              chatshahchat
        chachacha   chachacha
           shahchatshah
                shah
                shah
                  ha

cha
cha
chatcha
    cha
   shahcha
      cha
      chatcha
         cha
        shahcha
           cha
           cha

                      sh   ch
                      aha
                      ch   sh

EDWIN MORGAN

CHINESE CAT

pmrkgniaou
pmrkgniao
pmrkniao
pmrniao
pmriao
pmiao
miao
mao

EDWIN MORGAN

INSTAMATIC GLASGOW OCTOBER 1972

At the Old Ship Bank pub in Saltmarket
a milk-lapping contest is in progress.
A dozen very assorted Bridgeton cats
have sprung from their starting-blocks
to get their heads down in the gleaming saucers.
In the middle of the picture
young Tiny is about to win his bottle of whisky
by kittening through the sweet half-gill
in one minute forty seconds flat, but
Sarah, at the end of the line,
self-contained and silver-grey,
has sat down with her back to the saucer
and surveys the photographers calmly.
She is a cat who does not like milk.

EDWIN MORGAN

THE CAT

The cat noses among my books.
It nudges Homer.
Its wedge-shaped head nuzzles Tolstoy
to scratch at its fleas.
It pushes its head past Jane Austen searching for mice.
Later it sits on my knees
serene in the warm sunshine,
then in a trice
it runs out the window and climbs up a fresh green tree.
You too were a god, weren't you, cat,
tall, aloof, ghostly, impassive as Zeus.
You too are the justice of your own grass,
the doom of the mole and the mouse.

IAIN CRICHTON SMITH

CAT-FAITH

As a cat, caught by the door opening,
on the perilous top shelf, red-jawed and raspberry-clawed,
lets itself fall floorward without looking,
sure by cat-instinct it will find the ground,
where innocence is; and falls
anyhow, in a furball, so fast that the eye
misses the twist and trust
that come from having fallen before,
and only notices cat silking away,
crime inconceivable in so meek a walk:

so do we let ourselves fall morningward
through shelves of dream. When, libertine at dark,
we let the visions in, and the black window
grotesques us back, our world unbalances.
Many-faced monsters of our own devising
jostle on the verge of sleep, as the room
loses its edges and grows hazed and haunted
by words murmured or by woes remembered,
till, sleep-dissolved, we fall, the known world leaves us,
and room and dream and self and safety melt
into a final madness, where any landscape
may easily curdle, and the dead cry out . . .

but ultimately, it ebbs. Voices recede.
The pale square of the window glows and stays.
Slowly the room arrives and dawns, and we
arrive in our selves. Last night, last week, the past
leak back, awake. As light solidifies,
dream dims. Outside, the washed hush of the garden
waits patiently and, newcomers from death,
how gratefully we draw its breath!
Yet, to endure that unknown night by night,
must we not be sure, with cat-insight,
we can afford its terrors, and that full day
will find us at the desk, sane, unafraid—
cheeks shaven, letters written, bills paid?

ALASTAIR REID

PROPINQUITY

is the province of cats. Living by accident,
lapping the food at hand or sleeking down
in an adjacent lap when sleep occurs to them,
never aspiring to consistency
in homes or partners, unaware of property,
cats take their chances, love by need or nearness
as long as the need lasts, as long as the nearness
is near enough. The code of cats is simply
to take what comes. And those poor souls who claim
to own a cat, who long to recognise
in bland and narrowing eyes a look like love,
are bound to suffer should they expect
cats to come purring punctually home.
Home is only where the food and the fire are,
but might be anywhere. Cats fall on their feet,
nurse their own wounds, attend to their own laundry,
and purr at appropriate times. O folly, folly,
to love a cat, and yet

we dress with love the distance that they keep,
the hair-raising way they have, and easily blame
all their abandoned litters and torn ears
on some marauding tiger, well aware
that cats themselves do not care.
Yet part of us is cat. Confess—
love turns on accident and needs
nearness; and the various selves we have
accrue from our cat-wanderings, our chance
crossings. Imagination prowls at night,
cat-like, among odd possibilities.
Only our dog-sense brings us faithfully home,
makes meaning out of accident, keeps faith,
and, cat-and-dog, the arguments go at it.
But every night, outside, cat-voices call
us out to take a chance, to leave
the safety of our baskets and to let
what happens happen. 'Live, live!' they catcall.
'Each moment is your next! Propinquity,
propinquity is all!'

ALASTAIR REID

CURIOSITY

may have killed the cat. More likely,
the cat was just unlucky, or else curious
to see what death was like, having no cause
to go on licking paws, or fathering
litter on litter of kittens, predictably.

Nevertheless, to be curious
is dangerous enough. To distrust
what is always said, what seems,
to ask odd questions, interfere in dreams,
smell rats, leave home, have hunches,
does not endear cats to those doggy circles
where well-smelt baskets, suitable wives, good lunches
are the order of things, and where prevails
much wagging of incurious heads and tails.

Face it. Curiosity
will not cause us to die—
only lack of it will.
Never to want to see
the other side of the hill
or that improbable country
where living is an idyll
(although a probable hell)
would kill us all.
Only the curious
have if they live a tale
worth telling at all.

Dogs say cats love too much, are irresponsible,
are dangerous, marry too many wives,
desert their children, chill all dinner tables
with tales of their nine lives.

Well, they are lucky. Let them be
nine-lived and contradictory,
curious enough to change, prepared to pay
the cat-price, which is to die
and die again and again,
each time with no less pain.
A cat-minority of one
is all that can be counted on
to tell the truth; and what cats have to tell
on each return from hell
is this: that dying is what the living do,
and that dead dogs are those who never know
that dying is what, to live, each has to do.

ALASTAIR REID

A CAT

fastidious at each step
is nimble in mischance
though fearful of descent

a peacock in its grooming

obsessed by novelty
is unwearied in waiting
yet restless at a whim

a serpent in its gait

feigning indifference
is desolate when thwarted
then dawdles with its prey

an introvert in pleasure

scorning to be commanded
is servile in its begging
but gives of love unasked

an extrovert in hate.

GAEL TURNBULL

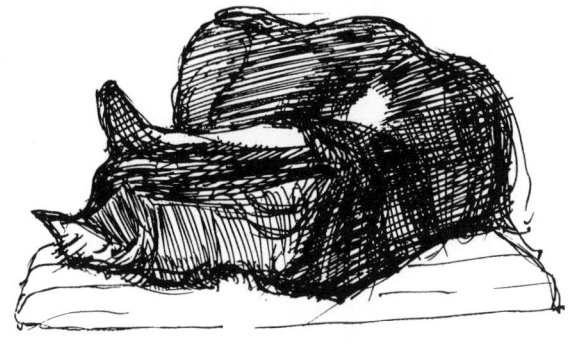

THE SPELL OF WATCHING

the
starlings land on the roof
they

worry the cat
who

stares out the window
she

opens her mouth

I
am anchored
I

cannot clap my hands

under the spell of watching

HAMISH WHYTE

CAT TALES

The ninth and final part of this anthology of Scottish writing on cats consists of a selection of stories past and present, from John Wilson's tale of rooftop caterwauling to the very modern account of a *menage à trois* in 'Mussolini' by Carl MacDougall. Robert McLellan's 'The Cat' may not be as terrifying as Poe's 'The Black Cat', surely the greatest of macabre cat tales, but is chilling nonetheless, its horror heightened by the homely setting and the matter-of-fact narration. As far as can be ascertained, this story and Walter Douglas Campbell's marvellous fairy story, 'Scratch Tom', have not been reprinted since their first appearance. They deserve to be better known.

A BATTLE OF CATS

Shepherd. Dinna fash wi' eisters the nicht, Mr Tickler—for this has been a stormy day, and they're no caller. Was ye dreamin, sir? For you seemed unco restless.

Tickler. I was, James.

Shepherd. What o'?

Tickler. A Battle of Cats.

'How sweet the moonlight sleeps upon the slates!'

Miss Tabitha having made an assignation with Tom Tortoiseshell, the feline phenomenon, they two sit curmurring, forgetful of mice and milk, of all but love! How meekly mews the Demure, relapsing into that sweet under-song—the Purr! And how curls Tom's whiskers like those of a Pashaw! The point of his tail—and the point only is alive—insidiously turning itself, with serpent-like seduction, towards that of Tabitha, pensive as a Nun. His eyes are rubies, hers emeralds—as they should be—his lightning, hers lustre—for in her sight he is the lord, and in his, she is the lady of Creation.

North.—

'O happy love!—where love like this is found!
O heartfelt raptures!—bliss beyond compare!
I've paced much this weary, mortal round,
And sage experience bids me this declare—
If Heaven a draught of heavenly pleasure spare,
One cordial in this melancholy vale,
'Tis when a youthful, loving, modest pair,
In other's arms breathe out the tender tale'—

Shepherd. The last line wunna answer—

'Beneath the milk-white thorn that scents the evening gale!'

Tickler. Woman or cat—she who hesitates is lost. But Diana, shining in heaven, the goddess of the Silver Bow, sees the peril of poor Pussy—and interposes her celestial aid to save the vestal. An enormous grimalkin, almost a wild cat, comes rattling along the roof, down from the chimney-top, and Tom Tortoiseshell, leaping from love to war, tackles the Red Rover in single combat. Sniff—snuff—splutter—squeak—squall—caterwaul, and throttle!

North. Where are the following lines?

> 'From the soft music of the spinning purr,
> When no stiff hair disturbs the glossy fur,
> The whining wail, so piteous and so faint,
> When through the house Puss moves with long complaint.
> To that unearthly throttling caterwaul,
> When feline legions storm the midnight wall,
> And chant, with short snuff and alternate hiss,
> The dismal song of hymeneal bliss'—

Shepherd. Wheesht, North—wheesht.

Tickler. Over the eaves sweeps the hairy hurricane. Two cats in one—like a prodigious monster with eight legs and a brace of heads and tails—and through among the lines on which clothes are hanging in the back-green, and which break the fall, the dual number plays squelch on the miry herbage.

Shepherd. A pictur o' a back-green in fowre words. I see it and them.

Tickler. The four-story fall has given them fresh fury and more fiery life. What tails! Each as thick as my arm, and rustling with electricity like the northern streamers. The Red Rover is generally uppermost—but not always—for Tom has him by the jugular like a very bulldog—and his small, sharp, tiger-teeth, entangled in the fur, pierce deeper and deeper into the flesh—while Tommy keeps tearing away at his rival, as if he would eat his way into his windpipe. Heavier than Tom Tortoiseshell is the Red Rover by a good many pounds; but what is weight to elasticity—what is body to soul? In the long tussle, the hero ever vanquishes the ruffian—as the Cock of the North the Gander.

North (bowing). Proceed.

Tickler. Cats' heads are seen peering over the tops of walls, and then their lengthening bodies, running crouchingly along the copestones, with pricked-up ears and glaring eyes, all attracted towards one common centre—the back-green of the inextinguishable battle. Some dropping, and some leaping down, from all altitudes, lo! a general *mêlée!* For Tabitha, having through a skylight forced her way down stairs, and out of the kitchen-window into the back-area, is sitting pensively on the steps,

> 'And like another Helen fires another Troy.'

Detachments come wheeling into the field of battle from all imaginable and unimaginable quarters—and you now see before you all the cats in Edinburgh, Stockbridge, and the suburbs, about as many, I should suppose, as the proposed constituents of our next city member.

Shepherd. The Town Council are naething to them in nummers. The back-green's absolutely composed o' cats.

Tickler. Up fly a thousand windows from ground-flat to attic, and what an exhibition of nightcaps! Here elderly gentlemen, apparently in their shirts, with head night-gear from Kilmarnock, worthy of Tappytoorie's self—behind them their wives—grandmothers at the least—poking their white faces, like those of sheeted corpses, over the shoulders of the fathers of their numerous progeny—there, chariest maids, prodigal enough to unveil their beauties to the moon, yet, in their alarm, folding the frills of their chemises across their bosoms— and lo! yonder the Captain of the Six Feet Club, with his gigantic shadow frightening that pretty damsel back to her couch, and till morning haunting her troubled dreams! 'Fire! Fire!' 'Murder! Murder!' is the cry—and there is wrath and wonderment at the absence of the police-officers and engines. A most multitudinous murder is in process of perpetration there—but as yet fire is there none; when lo! and hark! the flash and peal of musketry—and then the music of the singing slugs slaughtering the Catti, while bouncing up into the air, with Tommy Tortoise clinging to his carcass, the Red Rover yowls wolfishly to the moon, and then descending like lead into the stone-area, gives up his nine-ghosts, never to chew cheese more, and dead as a herring. In mid-air the Phenomenon had let go his hold, and seeing it in vain to oppose the yeomanry, pursues Tabitha, the innocent cause of all this woe, into the coal-cellar, and there, like Paris and Helen,

> 'When first entranced in Cranae's Isle they lay,
> Lip pressed to lip, and breathed their souls away,'

entitled but not tempted to look at a king, the peerless pair begin to purr and play in that subterranean paradise, forgetful of the pile of cat-corpses that in that catastrophe was heaped half-way up the currant-bushes on the walls, so indiscriminate had been the Strages. All undreamed of by them the beauty of the rounded moon, now hanging over the city, once more steeped in stillness and in sleep!

JOHN WILSON (CHRISTOPHER NORTH) (1785–1854)
'Noctes Ambrosianae', *Blackwood's Magazine*, April 1831

Note: 'Tickler' was Robert Sym, Wilson's uncle, and the Shepherd was, of course, the Ettrick Shepherd, James Hogg.

THE CAT

There were three grocers' shops in Kirkfieldbank, but I was best acquant wi Mistress Yuill's. It had been a guid shop at ae time, clean as a new preen and weill stockit, and whan I was a laddie haurdly auld eneuch for the schule I could hae thocht o naething better than the chance o cawin in wi a bawbee. It wasna juist for what ye could buy, but for the sicht and smell o it. She selt gey nearly everything ye could think o, frae paraffin and cheese to weekly papers and tacketty buits, and ye could hae spent a haill efternune peerin into aw the odd neuks at the faur end o the coonter, sniffin yer fill.

As time gaed bye, though, Mistress Yuill grew less able, and syne began to turn blin, and the last time I had cawed in the shop had been a fair disgrace, though the puir auld craitur couldna help it, nae dout. My first look at the winnock had gart me woner, for at ae end there was an auld grey cat sittin on a box o kippers, and at the tither a wheen sticks a gundie that the sun had meltit into ae big stickie mess.

I had come that day to Linmill for my simmer holiday, though, and Mistress Yuill's had aye been pairt o it, sae I didna let the winnock keep me oot. I liftit the sneck and pusht the door open.

The bell didna ping, and that was new tae. It gied a clatter like a pat lid. It was lood eneuch, for aw that, to hae brocht her forrit, but for a while there was nae sign o her, and I had rowth o time to hae a guid look roun.

It wasna plaisint. The flair was dirty and the coonter a fair clutter. Naething was fresh. The butter stank and the cheese was mouldie, and there was an auld ham-end aside the scales sae thick wi big blue flees that ye could hardly see it. The papers, weeks auld by the look o them, were aw markit. At first I thocht the cat had dune it, and the marks o its pads were on them shair eneuch, but on a closer look I foun finger-marks, hunders o them; and no juist on the papers. Aw ower the coonter, aw ower the haill shop, there were fingermarks, creeshie, flourie and aw sorts; and there was a look aboot them that wasna cannie.

The auld grey cat rase aff the kippers and cam in frae the winnock, slinkin alang wi its tail up, rubbin its backside on everything it passed and purrin like a kettle on the beyl. I followed its een and a cauld shiver cam ower me. Mistress Yuill had come forrit, hoo I dinna ken, and was feelin her wey alang the coonter, layin her hands on this and that, sweeties, puddens, papers and aw, and her blank blae een were like the shutters o a toom hoose.

'Ay?'

I stude like a gommeril. I could think o naething to ask for. The cat pat its back up and spat in my face.

'Ay?'

'A pair o whangs.'

It was aw I could think that wadna be foustie. They wad dae for my grandfaither.

The whangs were hingin frae a nail on a post that took the wecht o the upstairs flair. She felt alang the coonter for her knife, pawin the papers, and syne for the post, pawin the sweeties and puddens again. She ran her fingers ower the whangs to fin the ends o them. She cut aff twa.

'A penny.'

I pat the penny on the coonter and turnt to rin.

'Haud on,' she said.

She fingert the penny and let it drap on the coonter, listenin for the ring. It was a guid ane, nearly new. She felt for it, foun it, and haundit me the whangs.

'What is it?'

I couldna speak. Her een didna alter, but she soundit gey bitter.

'Ye're gey blate the day, Rab. Did ye think I wadna ken ye?'

Still I could say naething.

'Whan did ye stert usin whangs?'

'They're for my grandfaither.'

'Ay ay. Ye arena the first o the laddies to stop buyin sweeties.'

I backit and fell ower a pail. The cat lowpit doun aff the coonter and spat in my face again. I ran for the door.

I gied her shop the bye frae that day on, though whan my grandfaither drave me to Kirkfieldbank I couldna help but pass it, and ilka time I spied the winnock I grued at the sicht o the cat.

It was aboot twa months efter, whan the strawberries were bye and the blae plooms were turnin ripe, that I drave wi my grandfaither to Lanark to the Cattle Show. On oor wey through Kirkfieldbank he lat me haud the reyns, sae I didna look roun muckle except mebbe to see if the folk were watchin me, but as we passed Mistress Yuill's I gied a keek for the cat, for I couldna get it oot o my mind. I lay wauken aw nicht, whiles, thinkin o it, and aye whaun I foun mysell alane in the daurk I could see the wee nerra slits o its glintin green een.

The cat wasna there, or if it was it couldna be seen, for the shop was shuttert.

'Is it the hauf day, grandfaither?'

'Na.'

'Mistress Yuill's shop's shut.'

'Ay.'

'Is she no weill?'

'That's richt.'

'What's wrang wi her?'

'Naething.'

'There maun be something wrang if she's no weill.'

'Ay, there's something.'

'What is it?'

'She's deid, but dinna speak aboot it.'

'What wey that?'

'Dinna heed. Keep yer ee on the horse or I'll hae to tak the reyns mysell.'

That was eneuch. I didna press him. But the neist day, whan I was doun at the fute o the bottom orchard haein a look at the blae plooms, I met my kizzen Jockie, and he telt me his wey o it.

Aboot a fortnicht syne Mistress Yuill had grown sae desperate that she had peyed a laddie to come in and help her. I kent the laddie weill, for his mither had poued strawberries at Linmill. She didna pey him muckle, Mistress Yuill, but aw he had to dae was soop the flair and redd things up, and watch that naebody gied her a penny for a hauf-croun. He ran errands, tae, but there couldna hae been mony, for up to that she had sent oot the messages by a laddie frae the schule, efter fower o'clock.

Noo this laddie, Will MacPherson was his name, had watchit Mistress Yuill, day in day oot, till he foun oot whaur she hid the till key. She didna tak it hame, for she had a son bidin wi her, a deil for drink.

Then, ae daurk wat windy nicht, whan the Kirkfieldbank folk were sleepin, and there was nae soun bune the blatter o the wind and rain and the swish o Clyde watter, he had creepit roun to the shop back and sclimmed up on to a shed there. Frae the shed rufe he was able to wriggle up the sclaits o the shop itsell, and in the end he won to the skylicht abune the flair upstairs. There was a gey drap doun, but he maun hae managed it, for he foun the till key and fillled his pooches wi siller, as muckle as there was, and syne wi cigarettes and sweeties, though hoo he could hae stamacked the sweeties I dinna ken. Then he tried to fin his wey oot.

The skylicht was ower heich to grip frae the flair, sae he stude a chair aneth it and sclimmed up on to that. Still he couldna grip it, it seems, and he sclimmed up on to the chair back. It fell when he tried that, as ye wad hae thocht, but it maun hae served his turn, for he was able to pou himsell pairtly through. That was as faur as he gat, for to mak room for himsell he had putten the skylicht richt back on the sclaits, whaur it couldna be fastened.

The wind brocht it bash ower his heid.

The neist mornin Mistress Yuill gaed alang to the shop, and likely she missed him, and whether she gaed up the stair for something she keepit there, or whether she had second sicht like the lave o blin folk, naebody could say, but up the stair she gaed. She couldna hae seen the laddie, that was certain, sae she maun hae felt him wi her haunds.

He was hingin by the chin frae the skylicht, wi his airms stickin up oot through it.

She didna gang hame that nicht at her richt time, and her son didna bother, but a neibor that aye had her kettle beylin gat worrit, and gaed alang to the shop. The meenit she opened the door the cat flew at her. She gat aff wi a scart or twa and gaed for Galbraith, the polis. They had to throw a tattie bag ower it afore they could win in, and whan they gaed upstairs they foun Will MacPherson, wi Mistress Yuill on the flair at his feet. The shock had been ower muckle for her.

That was the story I heard frae my kizzen Jockie, but it wasna the trith. He hadna been telt richt himsell.

I gat the trith frae my faither, whan I was aulder, at Tam Baxter's funeral. Tam Baxter had been ane o the men to gang in wi Galbraith.

The laddie hadna filled his pooches wi siller at aw. He hadna haen the chance. Whan they had foun him hingin they had haurdly kent him. His claes were aw bluid and his face was like butcher-meat.

The cat had gaen for him the meenit he had landit on the flair.

Robert McLellan
(from No Scottish Twilight, ed M Lindsay and F Urquhart, 1947)

MUSSOLINI

Mussolini was a fine cat, found in a shop window. There was a sign, Kittens Free To Good Homes. I didn't have a good home, hardly any home at all, but I took him thinking he'd make a bad home better or at least improve my surroundings.

He snuggled into my jacket and sheltered from the wind. The traffic noises made him squeak, but we got back safely. He had a saucer of milk, explored the skirting boards, found the warmest place, slept and grew into a fine cat.

On the first morning, the first of many mornings, I made tea and toast while she read the paper, lying there languid and so beautiful she caught my breath, took it away. He came into the room and lay between us. The paper was boring, she exciting, so I melted into the warm tunnel and tickled her belly.

'Don't,' she said, but I knew she didn't mean it. 'Stop it. I'm reading.'

And Mussolini lay between us, staring at me, round eyes glazed and pleading: Who is she? What's wrong? What have I done? I could neither tickle her, nor throw him out. I knew he'd come back.

I remembered coming back to the house empty and cold and there he was, Mussolini, up at the window looking for me. When I opened the door he'd rub his face against my feet so I'd nearly trip over him. Mussolini purring and arching his back, telling me it was good to have me home: Hello, he'd say. Then he'd sit on the table after I'd fed him, while I was eating, doing nothing but looking at me and saying, Hello. And when I'd sit by the fire reading, up he'd pop, Mussolini coming up from nowhere to settle between me and the book, rubbing himself on the edge of the book till I stopped reading and stroked him, which could have gone on forever because he never got enough; but he knew when I'd had enough, for he'd settle, settle on my lap to let me read, even though I had to hold the book awkwardly as he purred while I read, sometimes fell asleep with the fire dying and him on my lap, Mussolini.

But now he was lying on the bed, wondering why. And as I was floating, just about to drift away, she slid down the bed, glided in beside me and said, 'Bloody cat,' as she pushed him away and leaned forward to kiss me. But he came back, like I knew he would, poked his face between our faces and burrowed between our noses, purring. She took her tongue out of my mouth and said, 'For God's sake,' as he dived into the space and lay there looking at me: Mussolini trying to tell me something, saying, What about me? Don't. Please. Don't. But she got up, naked, lifted him by the scruff of the neck, off the bed with his claws on the cover and threw him out the room into the hall then slammed the door as he scratched the paint, crying, Mussolini.

When I wakened she was stepping into her Marks and Spencer knickers and he was in the hall. He followed me around the place, but I was now over the top, beyond recall. I didn't want him running between my feet or interrupting my reading. Three days later he walked out. I went looking for him, but after five nights it rained and I didn't look any more.

Seventeen days and eighteen nights later he was back at the door. He ran a few steps and rolled on the carpet, saying, Hello, I'm back, Mussolini.

I suggested she feed him. 'Why?' she said. But she put down the plate, he ate the food and for the first time in his life asked for more.

Oh, we've all settled, but things have never been the same. Mussolini and I live in the same house now and that's about all. Sometimes, if I come into a room and say, 'How's it going, Musso?' he looks up. But he never holds the gaze; he looks up, turns away, closes his eyes or stares at the wall.

Mussolini staring at the wall.

CARL MacDougall
Sou'wester 3, December 1978

Potter and Siamese cat. Oscar Marzaroli

NO PLACE FOR PIBROCH

When MacTavish's bitch cat Dusky came home from the hill, after three days and nights away, he guessed what she'd been up to. He was right. When her kittens were due he watched her closely, but she outwitted him, and it took him five weeks to find them. By then they were furred balls of spitting, clawing fury. He drowned four of them, and kept one, which he took home, thinking he could tame it. He called it Pibroch.

But Pibroch would not be tamed. He grew more and more aloof from his mother, and closer and closer to Sandy the terrier, who accepted his toothing and clawing without growl or grimace. Everything else he attacked on sight. He killed hens and ducks: he attacked MacTavish's wife, ripping her forearm; he bit and clawed MacTavish's hand every time the stalker tried to woo him. Then one day, when he was about seven months old, he clawed MacTavish just below the right eye. 'That's it!' the stalker said. 'He'll hae tae go!' But when he came with the gun Pibroch had gone.

On the hill Pibroch changed dens daily until he found the disused eyrie of a golden eagle, which he made his lair. At night he hunted along the river banks, using a windblown spruce as a crossing place. At the beginning of the hind-shooting season, seeing men on the hill every morning with rifle and telescope, he gave up daylight hunting, and stayed close to the eyrie until dusk. Despite his upbringing he was as shy of men as the shyest wildcat on the hill.

From time to time he crossed tracks with a big vixen, sometimes at night, but usually when he was homing uphill in the morning. Halfway through the hind season he had two encounters with her that taught him all any cat needs to know about foxes.

He was lying outside the deer fence on a gusty, moonlit night when she came downwind behind him, which meant her nose was full of him while he could neither see nor smell her. If she hadn't dingled the bottom wire of the fence she would have had him for the chopping; but the sound warned him in time and he was on top of a rock outcrop before she reached the spot where he had been lying.

While she circled the outcrop, snarling up and sideways at him, he sat tall with bushed tail, wailing his war-cry and brandishing an armed forepaw. Once she leaped up at him, with teeth bared, but he met her with a forearm stroke that just missed her face and sent her back down to ponder.

She knew she had to get him down to do anything with him; up there he had the advantage, and could daub her face with blood, or have her eyes, before she could get near him with her teeth.

Each time she pawed up at him, with curled lip, he spat at her and hooked with that disconcerting forepaw. At last she turned away, as though inviting him to break when she wasn't looking, and Pibroch reacted so quickly that he took her by surprise. He was halfway to the deer fence before she could get into her stride, and on top of a post, spitting at her, when she reached the bottom.

Nervous and jittery, he didn't come down from his perch until long after the fox had gone. He hunted no more that night; instead he went straight back to his bed in the eyrie, and fell asleep almost at once. In the morning he saw no fox.

But she was after him now—cat-hunting: a cat killer who had little respect for the genuine cat of the mountains, even less for half-breeds, and none at all for house cats, however formidable.

Pibroch was lazing in the eyrie, with a freshly killed rabbit beside him, when he saw her padding uphill towards the crag. His bristling was reflex, and at first he wasn't alarmed; then he saw her on the sheepwalk and knew she was coming to the eyrie.

He met her on the threshold—flat-eared, crouched down—trying to scare her off, with his weight on his right forefoot and his left hooking towards her face. She chopped at him, keeping her face well back from his clawing left-handers, and it was obvious she was coming right on. Pibroch backed away, hissing explosively, and changing feet to swipe with his right forepaw. The vixen kept coming, sure of him now. Yet she had miscalculated.

To a fox, the way into the eyrie had to be the way out. But not to a cat.

Just when she thought she had him—when she was ready to paw-whip him—he daunted her momentarily with wild skelloch and two-fisted threat; then, before she could kep him, he was scrambling up the rock face, clawing with hind- and fore-feet to the top of the overhang. From there he bounded on to a narrow shelf where no fox could hope to reach him. And there he stood, slit-eyed, with back arched and tail bushed, until the vixen acknowledged defeat and skulked away—with his rabbit in her jaws!

Pibroch didn't return to the eyrie. In the timber, high above the river and close to the deer fence, he found a cleft in an outcrop of rock that opened into a roomy cavity where a tawny owl had reared three owlets earlier in the year. There he denned up, while the blizzards swept the hill and drifted the snow against the deer fence.

Hungry stags broke into the timber on the heels of a storm, which was fortunate for Pibroch, for they trampled out his tracks, so that he was missed by MacTavish when he came with the shepherd from time to time to look for sheep in the drifts along the deer fence.

Rabbits and white hares were his standby during the lean days, although he killed a hen capercaillie in the timber and two red grouse on the hill. One morning, during a thaw, he was padding downhill towards the deer fence, with his fur wet and his pads bleached, when he came on the forequarters of a hind that had been killed by poachers. Bellying down, he ate slowly and gorged, liking the venison as most cats do at first eating. When the scavenging ravens arrived he withdrew to a mossed stump to clean his fur and face, pausing every now and again to watch the birds tearing at the carcase.

There were six of them croaking and squawking over it when the hen eagle came down. She flap-walked to the carcase, driving the ravens back. By the time Pibroch was ready to leave she was on top of it, tearing at the meat while the ravens stood around, croaking and blinking, waiting for her to finish. Pibroch returned later to the venison and ate his fill, before the carrion birds came back to strip the carcase clean.

The eagles were making up their nest on the crag when Pibroch met the she wildcat from the Fiddler's Cairn. Snow was still lying on the high ground, and in the dark corries, but all the low ground was clear.

The big cat was yowling her eerie lovesong from the rocks below the snowline, summoning a mate, and Pibroch padded uphill to tryst with her. But she was dubious about him, and greeted him with such a dis-play of fireworks—hissing, spitting, screeching and clawing the air— that he drew back, daunted, and sat down to see what she would do.

She kept up her caterwauling and Pibroch, finding his voice, tried to match her display with a sobbing, quavering coronach of his own. Almost at once a third voice yowled and crackled in challenge, and a big wild tom came leaping down through the rocks, with ears flat and teeth bared to the gums, swallowing his breath in choking sobs, wailing, and hissing explosively like fired greenstick.

The she-cat bellied down, flat-eared, singing through her nose, and watched the wild tom bouncing sideways towards Pibroch. As in his turavees with Dusky, Pibroch leaped sideways to meet the attack with all his claws unsheathed to grapple, but before he could deliver even a parrying stroke the wildcat struck and held. He gripped Pibroch with his foreclaws, turned over on his back, and began ripping with his eviscerating hindfeet.

This was cat-fighting: a style instinctively understood by Pibroch. But in a grapple of this kind he was completely outmatched in weight and weapons. The treading claws ripped his belly fur; the big tusks bit at his neck. Pibroch was being hurt, and not liking it. When they broke apart, after a grappling roll downhill, he bounded clear and fled.

He fled downhill to the river, and crossed by the fallen spruce. Near the edge of the forest he found an ancient tree with a hollow heart. Deep in the cavity a tawny owl was dozing on three eggs. Pibroch, aching and bleeding, and needing a dark corner where he could rest and mend, clawed his way up to the hole and glared down at the brooding owl. She stared back at him, clicking her beak, but when the armed forepaw reached down she scrambled clear by a second exit and leaped long-legged into the night, *keewicking* in anger and alarm.

Soon her mate was flying around with her. They flew down to the hole many times in the night, but Pibroch slept, unheeding. At noon he awoke, irked by a commanding thirst. When he appeared at the entrance the owls flew at him, but he fended them off, then climbed stiffly to the ground. The hen owl flew in to the nest. Seeing her eggs still there she tumbled headlong in and, after much shuffling and turning about, settled down to incubate.

That spring Pibroch denned in a cairn above the tree line, and each dusk he hunted below the screes and along the edge of the forest, killing voles and mice, hares and rabbits, grouse, plovers and moss cheepers. He grew visibly. He put on muscle and his fur took on a rich bloom. He became more and more like a true wildcat in build and temperament. But he was an outlaw; a beast of fire and brimstone, with all gentleness dead in him.

He was also lucky.

At fox-time the terriers sniffed at the cairn without interest because Pibroch wasn't at home. MacTavish guessed they were smelling mouse or stoat because there had never been anything of a size in the cairn before. So they all left without closer look, while Pibroch, gorged tight on a blackcock, was dreaming cat-dreams in a hollow tree in the forest, unmolested by an owl who now had three owlets in the branches, all successfully hatched from eggs that had been warmed for a night and most of a day by a cat.

There was no smell of dogs when he returned to the cairn, so he stayed on there, and his luck held. There was no fox den in the area so no one came back looking for one. By day and night he moved freely, molested by none. Until the eagle took an interest in him.

For more than two months she had been thirled to the eyrie, where she now had twin eaglets three weeks old. She had more time now to perch above the nest and preen and look around. One day she saw Pibroch and flew down to look at him.

He was making his way to the river when he heard the swoosh of wings overhead. He had no idea what an eagle was but sensed that the sound was dangerous. He didn't look up; thus he saved his eyes. Nor did he leap to meet the assault; thus he saved his life. Instead, he flattened, turned, and doubled back, so that the eagle overshot, her mightly talons gripping heather but no cat-fur.

The eagle threw up heavily, with mighty buffet of wings; then she turned and came in again, with feathered legs outstretched and talons clutching like grappling irons. But Pibroch was now under a rock, with his fur on end, wailing his war-song, and the eagle, thwarted, flapped heavily on to the rock. She folded her wings, and glared fiercely down at the spot where the cat had been. Maybe she knew he was under the rock; maybe she had already forgotten about him. Certainly it didn't occur to her to search for him. Before long she ruffled her feathers, spread wide her wings, and launched out across the glen to the eyrie.

Pibroch denned in the cairn all summer and into the autumn. Snow fell early that year, and when the hills were white he moved down into the glen, and found a warm den among rocks near the fallen spruce. The next night he used the spruce as a bridge, leaving a neat set of prints in the snow. Before a fresh fall came to hide them they were seen and recognised by the under-keeper, who was a great one for the trapping.

The man came back in the afternoon and set a gin in the middle of the spruce trunk. He anchored it so that the chain would reach the water. Then he brushed away the snow on both sides of the set and left with his dogs.

No mountain fox with eyes in his head, or a nose that could still smell, would have walked within five yards of such a set. But Pibroch came padding along the bank, picked his way along the trunk, and walked right into it.

The trap clicked and Pibroch yowled an unearthly yowl that started the ravens croaking and the grey crows talking in the timber. When he tried to leap away he was pulled up short, and fell with the trap into the river. He couldn't spring back because of the weight of the trap; and he couldn't swim away because he was held by the chain. And soon he would have drowned.

That's the way it should have been: the way it was meant to be. But it didn't happen to Pibroch. The jaws of the trap hadn't closed cleanly, and eased off more and more as he struggled. When his lungs were already half full of water he suddenly found himself free. Half-dead, coughing and spitting, he struck out weakly and managed to drift ashore, leaving only fur and skin in the trap.

But his paw was painful and bleeding, and the cold irked the wound. By morning the foot had swollen to the size of two, and he couldn't put his weight on it. So he was unable to hunt.

All day he slept fitfully, and all the following night, but still he was a cripple, lick-licking to assuage the anguish in his foot. He licked snow to quench his thirst, but could do nothing to soothe the hunger in his belly.

The sun shone brightly at noon, and the white sparkled on the hills. Blue shadows lay aslant the ridges facing the light. Pibroch came out of his bed, yawned, then began to hirple downhill on three legs, heading for the stalking road leading into the forest. When he reached the road he began to follow it down through the timber, limping along a wheel rut, and stopping every now and again to lick his wound.

He was headed for MacTavish's cottage.

The dogs in the kennels set up an uproar of barking when they winded him in the bushes outside the yard, and MacTavish came to the window to find out the cause. When he saw, he opened the door. Past him, before he could stop him, rushed Sandy the terrier: Sandy the foxer, with an abiding hatred of all cats except his own. Deaf to the cries of MacTavish he rushed to the worry.

Pibroch bounded three-legged into a rhododendron thicket, and there the two met—the half-wild cat and the snarling terrier who had once been his friend—unseen by the stalker or his wife. Unable to strike with a forepaw, Pibroch tried to turn on his back to fight in the only way he knew. But Sandy was too quick for him. The white teeth flashed and chopped, and in a moment the big cat was dead, with a rumbling terrier straddling his body.

MacTavish forced his way into the thicket and picked up the tawny, broken body. Shaking his head sorrowfully he carried it to his wife.

'It's Pibroch,' he said. 'Sair hurted in a trap looks like. He needed fixing. Well, Sandy's fixed him all right. But maybe it's for the best. There was nae place for him oot there, and there was certainly nane for him here.'

DAVID STEPHEN
The Scotsman, 30 December 1980

THE KITTEN

The feet were tramping directly towards her. In the hot darkness under the tarpaulin the cat cuffed a kitten to silence and listened intently.

She could hear the scruffling and scratching of hens about the straw-littered yard; the muffled grumbling of the turning churn in the dairy; the faint clink and jangle of harness from the stable—drowsy, comfortable, reassuring noises through which the clang of the iron-shod boots on the cobbles broke ominously.

The boots ground to a halt, and three holes in the cover, brilliant, diamond-points of light, went suddenly black. Crouching, the cat waited, then sneezed and drew back as the tarpaulin was thrown up and glaring white sunlight struck at her eyes.

She stood over her kittens, the fur of her back bristling and the pupils of her eyes narrowed to pin-points. A kitten mewed plaintively.

For a moment, the hired man stared stupidly at his discovery, then turned towards the stable and called harshly: 'Hi, Maister! Here a wee.'

A second pair of boots clattered across the yard, and the face of the farmer, elderly, dark and taciturn, turned down on the cats.

'So that's whaur she's been,' commented the newcomer slowly.

He bent down to count the kittens and the cat struck at him, scoring a red furrow across the back of his wrist. He caught her by the neck and flung her roughly aside. Mewing she came back and began to lick her kittens. The Master turned away.

'Get rid of them,' he ordered. 'There's ower many cats aboot this place.'

'Aye, Maister,' said the hired man.

Catching the mother, he carried her, struggling and swearing, to the stable, flung her in, and latched the door. From the loft he secured an old potato sack and with this in his hand returned to the kittens.

There were five, and he noticed their tigerish markings without comprehending as, one by one, he caught them and thrust them into the bag. They were old enough to struggle, spitting, clawing and biting at his fingers.

Throwing the bag over his shoulder he stumped down the hill to the burn, stopping twice on the way to wipe the sweat that trickled down his face and neck, rising in beads between the roots of his lint-white hair.

Behind him, the buildings of the farm-steading shimmered in the heat. The few trees on the slope raised dry, brittle branches towards a sky bleached almost white. The smell of the farm, mingled with peat-reek, dung, cattle, milk, and the dark tang of the soil, was strong in his nostrils, and when he halted there was no sound but his own breathing and the liquid burbling of the burn.

Throwing the sack on the bank, he stepped into the stream. The water was low, and grasping a great boulder in the bed of the burn he strained to lift it, intending to make a pool.

He felt no reluctance at performing the execution. He had no feelings about the matter. He had drowned kittens before. He would drown them again.

Panting with his exertion, the hired man cupped water between his hands and dashed it over his face and neck in a glistening shower. Then he turned to the sack and its prisoners.

He was in time to catch the second kitten as it struggled out of the bag. Thrusting it back and twisting the mouth of the sack close, he went after the other. Hurrying on the sun-browned grass, treacherous as ice, he slipped and fell headlong, but grasped the runaway in his outflung hand.

It writhed round immediately and sank needle-sharp teeth into his thumb, so that he grunted with pain and shook it from him. Unhurt, it fell by a clump of whins and took cover beneath them.

The hired man, his stolidity shaken by frustration, tried to follow. The whins were thick and, scratched for his pains, he drew back, swearing flatly, without colour or passion.

Stooping, he could see the eyes of the kitten staring at him from the shadows under the whins. Its back was arched, its fur erect, its mouth open, and its thin lips drawn back over its tiny white teeth.

The hired man saw, again without understanding, the beginnings of tufts on the flattened ears. In his dull mind he felt a dark resentment at this creature which defied him. Rising, he passed his hand up his face in heavy thought, then slithering down to the stream, he began to gather stones. With an armful of small water-washed pebbles he returned to the whins.

First he strove to strike at the kitten from above. The roof of the whins was matted and resilient. The stones could not penetrate it. He flung straight then—to maim or kill—but the angle was difficult and only one missile reached its mark, rebounding from the ground and striking the kitten a glancing blow on the shoulder.

Kneeling, his last stone gone, the hired man watched, the red in his face deepening and thin threads of crimson rising in the whites of his eyes as the blood mounted to his head. A red glow of anger was spreading through his brain. His mouth worked and twisted to an ugly rent.

'Wait—wait,' he cried hoarsely, and, turning, ran heavily up the slope to the trees. He swung his whole weight on a low-hanging branch, snapping it off with a crack like a gun-shot.

Seated on the warm, short turf, the hired man prepared his weapon, paring at the end of the branch till the point was sharp as a dagger. When it was ready he knelt on his left knee and swung the branch to find the balance. The kitten was almost caught.

The savage lance-thrust would have skewered its body as a trout is spiked on the beak of a heron, but the point, slung too low, caught in a fibrous root and snapped off short. Impotently the man jabbed with his broken weapon while the kitten retreated disdainfully to the opposite fringe of the whins.

In the slow-moving mind of the hired man the need to destroy the kitten had become an obsession. Intent on this victim, he forgot the others abandoned by the burn side; forgot the passage of time, and the hard labour of the day behind him. The kitten, in his distorted mind, had grown to a monstrous thing, centring all the frustrations of a brutish existence. He craved to kill. . . .

But so far the honours lay with the antagonist.

In a sudden flash of fury the man made a second bodily assault on the whins and a second time retired defeated.

He sat down on the grass to consider the next move as the first breath of the breeze wandered up the hill. As though that were the signal, in the last moments of the sun, a lark rose, close at hand, and mounted the sky on the flood of its own melody.

The man drank in the coolness thankfully, and, taking a pipe from his pocket, lit the embers of tobacco in the bowl. He flung the match from him, still alight, and a dragon's tongue of amber flame ran over the dry grass before the breeze, reached a bare patch of sand and flickered out. Watching it, the hired man knitted his brows and remembered the heather-burning, and mountain hares that ran before the scarlet terror. And he looked at the whins.

The first match blew out in the freshening wind, but at the second the bush burst into crackling flame.

The whins were alight on the leeward side and burned slowly against the wind. Smoke rose thickly, and sparks and lighted slivers of wood sailed off on the wind to light new fires on the grass of the hillside.

Coughing as the pungent smoke entered his lungs, the man circled the clump till the fire was between him and the farm. He could see the kitten giving ground slowly before the flame. He thought for a moment of lighting this side of the clump also and trapping it between two fires; took his matches from his pocket, hesitated, and replaced them. He could wait.

Slowly, very slowly, the kitten backed towards him. The wind fought for it, delaying, almost holding the advance of the fire through the whins.

Showers of sparks leaped up from the bushes that crackled and spluttered as they burned, but louder than the crackling of the whins, from the farm on the slope of the hill, came another noise—the clamour of voices. The hired man walked clear of the smoke that obscured his view and stared up the hill.

The thatch of the farmhouse, dry as tinder, was aflare.

Gaping, he saw the flames spread to the roof of the byre, to the stables; saw the farmer running the horses to safety, and heard the thunder of hooves as the scared cattle, turned loose, rushed from the yard. He saw a roof collapse in an uprush of smoke and sparks, while a kitten, whose sire was a wild cat, passed out of the whins unnoticed and took refuge in a deserted burrow.

From there, with cold, defiant eyes, it regarded the hired man steadfastly.

ALEXANDER REID
(from *Scottish Short Stories*, ed F Urquhart, 1957)

SCRATCH TOM

It was indeed a dreary November evening, and the wind, herald of the coming winter, swept round the lonely cottage on the moor. Within, a poor old dame sat cowering over the fast-dying embers of a few sticks, the last her feeble strength was able to collect.

It had been a wretched season; the root-crop had failed, her goat had died of disease, and now, without money and without friends— but a half-burnt faggot to warm and a mouldy bannock to sustain her—she looked forward to the future with terror and despair. Desolation ruled within, and the wind seemed to moan a dirge without.

Poor old thing! she gave a last stir to the fast-dying embers, placed her wretched bannock on the platter at her side, and drew her thin, faded shawl around her shivering limbs. With a habit born of many a day's task, she stretched out her hand to the old spinning-wheel at her side. Alas! here another disappointment presented itself: there was no wool to spin or flax to card. All had gone, like food and fuel, long ago. Still, she drew it towards her, and moved the treadle with her foot, for its monotonous beat seemed to soothe her, like the voice of an old friend sympathising, though helpless as herself.

What is that faint cry at the door, accompanied by a dull scratching on the threshold? Can there be another creature more wretched this night than herself, that it seeks for charity at the hand of a poor old dame?

At any rate, the Whatever-it-was had to be admitted, and, opening the door, the kind old woman, forgetful for a moment of her own wants in the pity for another's, let in from the darkness something like the shadow of a shade. So thin, so bony, so gaunt was this creature which crept along the floor and squatted down on the hearthstone at her feet, that it seemed but some dried branch blown in by the wind.

Its tail hung down like a frozen cord; its ears, like withered leaves, drooped painfully from a seemingly skinless skull; hardly a piece of fur covered its emaciated anatomy; it seemed nought but teeth and claws and eyes. Eyes large as saucers, green as emeralds, these were the only things that revealed it to the old dame as a starving cat.

'Poor creature!' said she; 'so there is something worse off than myself at this moment in the world, though I would scarcely have believed that possible. What is your name, creature?' said she.

'Scratch Tom,' said the cat.

'I did not ask you what I was to do,' said she, 'but what your name is, creature.'

'Scratch Tom,' said the cat.

'Well, if you wish it, I will,' said the dame; and she stroked the cat from head to tail, and—would you believe it?—something like the ghost of a purr came from somewhere.

'So there's something more bony than myself,' said the dame, as she stroked the cat, 'though I scarcely would have thought so.

'And would you like a piece of bannock?' said she. Skulls and cross-bones! what a squeal of assent came from between the teeth of the cat! The wife nearly fell over backward from fright.

So she gave it a piece of cake. There was one snap, and the bit was swallowed; the wife had to draw back her fingers swiftly to prevent them being snapped up too.

'So there's something more hungry in this world than myself,' said she, 'though I never would have believed that possible.

'Well then, take it all,' said the dame; 'it may satisfy you, poor thing, and it would only keep starvation from me for a few hours longer at the best.'

So she threw the cat the remainder of the bannock. It was stale, and broke into three fragments as it struck the floor.

The cat ate the first bit, and it swelled and grew to the size of the dame's footstool.

The cat ate the second bit, and it swelled and grew to the size of the dame's chair.

The cat ate the third bit, and it swelled and grew to the size of the dame's wooden table. And a more plump and well-furred cat you could not have seen had you searched the town of Kirkcaldy from one end to the other.

'Now,' said the cat—for of course you have already perceived it was a fairy cat, not a common one—'you have given me your all, and you took pity on a poor starving cat when in want yourself. You shall have your reward, if you only do as I bid you.'

Well, the dame was not slow to promise that, you may be sure.

'Get on my back,' said the cat, 'and we will seek a fortune in the Caves of Darkness.'

'But I shall fall off,' said the dame; 'for I am weak, and not used to riding.'

'Tie your apron under my body,' said the cat, 'and hold on tight by the strings.'

So the wife did as she was bid; she tied her apron under the cat's body, and, seating herself on its back, held tight to the strings.

'Now, off we go,' said the cat; 'say no more than, but say all that I bid you; do no more than, but do all that I tell you.' And the dame promised.

Into the dark night went the cat and his burden, and if the wind blew fierce and wild, it was the cat that won the race and left it shrieking far behind, nor did he draw breath till he arrived at a great rock in the side of a great hill with a great door in the centre, studded over with bolts of iron, and hung on hinges of living snakes that curled round and round the granite door-posts on either side.

Here the cat turned, and, bidding the dame dismount, he struck the door with a violent kick, till the great timbers shook and rattled, and the thunder echoed in the mountains.

'Who knocks so loud?' said a voice within.

'The Princess of the Land of Light and her servant, Scratch Tom,' said the cat.

'We have heard of neither before, and before I open the gate you must give me the sign,' said the voice.

'Put your hand under the door, and I will give you the sign,' said the cat.

Then there appeared under the door a long, bony, and hairy arm, like an ape's, with long red and green claws, which shone and glistened in the moonlight.

In a trice the cat had seized the arm between his teeth, and held so fast he drew blood with his fangs.

'Let go!' said the voice. 'Let go!'

'Not till you put the key under the gate,' said the cat.

So the key was pushed under the gate, and the cat let the arm go.

'Now,' said the cat to the dame, 'take this key and stand on my back, and turn it in the lock.'

So the cat arched its back till it was just so high that the dame, standing on tiptoe, could put the key in the lock.

'Don't let the key go, for your life's sake!' said the cat. So the dame turned the key in the lock, which gave a groan like a dying monster, and then, pulling it out, she hid it under her shawl.

'Now, push,' said the cat. So the dame pushed and the cat pushed, and the cat pushed and the dame pushed, till the timbers rattled, and the iron knobs shook, and the snake hinges wriggled again and again, but the door would not open.

'Take three hairs out of my tail,' said the cat, 'and stroke the nose of the snake-hinge in the centre.'

The dame did so, and the snake gave so fierce a twist that the great door flew open of its own accord.

'Now, give me my key,' said the voice.

'The Princess of the Land of Light takes no service without giving a reward in return,' said the cat. 'I will whisper to you how the Trolls brew heather beer on Morven.'

Now the voice wanted the key back, and also it was anxious to know the secret of heather beer, so it stretched its head down close to the cat's, who swiftly bit it off.

Then they stuffed the voice's body under the gate to prevent it from shutting, and the dame, mounting, took up her apron-strings, and off they went to the Caves of Darkness, where the black east wind ever blows.

Away and away into the gloom went the cat and his burden, and if the wind blew fierce and wild, it was the cat that won the race and left it shrieking far behind.

Suddenly, without giving warning, the cat stopped, so that it almost brought the dame over its ears, and said, 'Place your hand behind my left ear, and scratch Tom.'

And the dame did so, and oh! it was the brightness of the moon that came from the cat's head, and filled a great space around with dazzling light.

The dame found herself in an immense hall that seemed built of black marble, and round it there were galleries on galleries, one above the other, mounting innumerable to a roof that stretched upward and upward till lost in a black cloudland above. In these galleries were seated in rows, one behind the other, thousands on thousands of strange beings of human shape, but of giant height, clothed in robes of silver scales, with caps on their heads, each cap made of a single ruby, ruddy as blood. Every head was adorned with large yellow parchment ears, tipped with green fur; while under each forehead were enormous eyes like white toadstools, circular and convex, bulging, rolling, and blinking in the unaccustomed glare, while every hairy neck was stretched a yard long into the great space of the hall below.

The King of the Dark Caverns sat at the further end of the hall on a throne of black marble, carved like a shell, and encrusted with golden stars. His robe was of the black swansdown, overlaid with a network of pearls, and his crown was made of one pearl, with a plume above of the feathers of the black sea-cormorant. Beside him sat the princess, dressed in a garment of gold threads worked crosswise. Her crown was a single diamond, shaped as the crescent moon, and her hands and feet were incased in gloves and shoes studded with lustrous jewels. King, and princess too, had large parchment ears and toadstool eyes, and they both eyed the strangers, and stretched their long hairy necks a full yard towards the dame and Scratch Tom.

'Who are ye?' said the king, in a voice of thunder, 'you that dare intrude into the realms of the King of the Dark Caverns?'

'Say "I am the Princess of the Plains of Light,"' said the cat to the dame, '"and this is my servant Scratch Tom."'

The dame said so.

'How do you make the bright light?' said the king.

'Say "That is my secret,"' said the cat.

And the dame said so.

'It's perfectly lovely,' said the princess.

'Perfectly beautiful,' echoed the whole assembly.

'Can you make it any brighter?' said the princess.

'Put your left hand under my chin,' said the cat, 'and scratch Tom.'

And the dame did so, and oh! it was the brightness of the sun that came from the cat's head, and filled the great hall around with dazzling light.

'Too bright, too bright!' shrieked the princess, and the whole crowd covered their toadstool eyes with their parchment ears, which flapped together on their foreheads with the sound of a million snuff-boxes being shut by a million thumbs, and they drew back their heads behind their shoulders.

'Put your right hand under my chin and scratch Tom,' said the cat.

And the dame did so, and oh! it was again as the brightness of the moon.

'That's much better,' said the princess. 'Much better,' shouted the vast crowd, and they lifted their parchment ears from their toadstool eyes, and blinked and rolled them again, and stretched their long hairy necks a full yard towards the dame and Scratch Tom.

'What will you take for your secret?' said the King of the Dark Caverns.

'Say, "To be your queen,"' said the cat; and the dame said so.

'That cannot be,' said the King of the Dark Caverns; but all the crowd were so delighted with the brightness that they clamoured and howled, till the king was frightened, and said it should be so. So they prepared a chair of state for the dame beside the king. 'Now come and be my queen,' said the King of the Dark Caverns.

'Say "No,"' said the cat, '"not till I have the crown of the single diamond that is on the head of the princess."'

And the dame said so.

'That cannot be,' said the King of the Dark Caverns; but all the crowd were so delighted with the brightness that they clamoured and howled till the king was frightened, and said it should be so.

So they gave the crown made of the single diamond to the dame, and the princess, when she saw the crown taken away, wept tears of anger which fizzed like molten lead as they fell upon the pavement below the throne. But the dame placed the diamond crown underneath her shawl.

'Put your hand under my right ear,' said the cat, 'and scratch Tom.'

The dame did so, and in one moment the great hall was in complete darkness.

'Now hold on tight,' said the cat; and into the darkness went the cat and his burden; and if the wind followed fierce and wild, it was the cat that won the race and left it shrieking far behind.

But the dame was uneasy, what with the crown of a single diamond, and the great key of the gate which she had to keep below her shawl, and in thinking about these she forgot to hold on to the apron-strings. To steady herself, she unwittingly laid hold of the cat by the left ear, and in doing so she gave the cat a scratch. It was the least little scratch in the world, but it was quite sufficient for harm, for in an instant there was again the bright light of the moon shining from the cat's head throughout the cavern, and, to her intense horror, she saw behind her the creatures of the cavern, headed by their king, in hot pursuit with scimitars of steel and long forks shod with sharp and barbed fishhooks, and they yelled in triumph as they rushed upon the fugitives.

'Put your left hand under my right ear,' said the cat, 'and scratch Tom; and be quick about it, or we are lost.'

And the dame did so.

Instantly they were plunged into darkness, and the cat and his burden fled into the gloom, till the yells of the pursuers grew fainter and fainter in the distance.

'If you make a mistake like that again we are done for,' said the cat.

'Trust me for that,' said the dame.

And now they arrived at the door of the cavern, and there, at the cat's bidding, the dame dismounted.

'Pull the body of the voice from under the door,' said the cat.

And the dame did so.

Now, push!' said the cat, 'and let us close the door.' So the cat pushed and the dame pushed, and the dame pushed and the cat pushed, till the iron knobs shook and the snake-hinges wriggled again and again; but the door would not shut. And the yells of the pursuers grew louder and louder in the distance.

'Take three hairs out of my tail,' said the cat, 'and strike the nose of the snake-hinge in the centre.'

Now the dame was so nervous and in such a hurry, that instead of three hairs, she more likely pulled three hundred out from the cat's tail! At any rate, it was quite a handful she applied to the snake's nose, and in consequence the snake-hinge gave such a frantic wriggle that the door flew to before the dame and the cat could get clear of the passage; so, although they themselves managed to get beyond the doorway, the cat's tail and the dame's skirts were firmly wedged between the door and the gate-post.

And the yells of the pursuers grew louder and louder and louder, for they were now at the inner side of the door.

'There's no time to be lost,' said the cat, and he turned round and bit his tail off, and tore the dame's dress in two pieces.

'Now,' said the cat to the dame, 'take the key and get on my back, and turn the key in the lock'; and the cat arched its back till it was just so high that the dame, standing on tiptoe, could put the key in the lock, and the dame turned the key.

'Pull the key out,' said the cat.

'I can't,' said the dame.

'Then leave it where it is,' said the cat; 'and quick! get on my back and let us flee!'

For by this time strange things began to crawl underneath the gate, hairy arms with scimitars, and forks shod with fishhooks, that waved about blindly and wildly, striking at their prey.

And the yells of the pursuers grew yet ever louder, and there were scratchings and bitings, and gnawing and kicking, till it seemed as if the gate itself must come down.

But the foolish old dame thought that she would try just once more to get the key out of the lock, and that delay almost cost them their lives; for now bolts began to fly out from the great gate, and the timbers fell cracking and splintering in all directions; the savage yells grew fiercer and fiercer, and the snake-hinges were strained almost to bursting.

So the dame left the key in the lock, and leaped down, for she was in terror at the tumult. But, alas! it was not soon enough, for one of the forks with fishhooks caught her dress; and, as she turned to loosen it, yet another and another fixed itself in her garment, and it was no use for the cat to bite and tear at them, for as soon as he broke one or tore another, more came and encircled the dame in their dreadful grip.

And it was twilight outside the gate, for the sun had not yet risen.

Then with a crash the great gate fell, and the snakes and bolts and timbers burst into a thousand fragments, and there, crowding the mouth of the cavern, the unnumbered hosts of the King of the Dark Caverns stood brandishing their cruel weapons and rolling their toadstool eyes, waiting but for one moment to give a triumphant squall of victory before they rushed in their thousands upon their exhausted and seemingly helpless prey.

With a superhuman effort the cat tore the dame out of the network of fishhooks that held her fast, and seizing her in his teeth, with scarcely a shred of clothing left upon her, he dashed with his burden down the precipice.

But it was of no use. If the cat could leave the wind behind, he could not escape the wild whirlwind of pursuit that fury and vengeance now urged on. Soon the cat found himself hemmed in by the cavern monsters on every side; so escape by flight being impossible, he turned at bay, and placed the dame on the ground and stood above her, lightning flashing from his eyes, and blood and foam dripping from his jaws.

And it was twilight on the battlefield, for the sun had not yet risen.

Like a paladin of old the cat kept up the unequal fight. Forks, fishhooks, scimitars, claws, arms, eyes, and even heads, that approached too near, were crushed, broken, and bitten off by the jaws and fangs of Scratch Tom. His head seemed to whirl round and be in every direction, no matter from what quarter the attack came; but numbers on numbers pressed from behind to fill the places of those disabled in front, till at last a great rampart of torn bodies and broken weapons made a dreadful circle round the cat and the now unconscious dame.

The sky above seemed a wavy network of quivering swords and whirling hooks. The enemy, gathering themselves for one last tremendous effort, pressed up the sides of the rampart in a wild, frenzied rush of hideous determination and fury. Woe's me for the dame and her defender! Even the magic cat is getting exhausted, for what magic may withstand so overwhelming an onslaught?

And the winter morning twilight still lay dim over the fearful strife.

But just as the surging mass reached the top of the incline, it stood still, for a loud voice, that rang above the tumult, bid them Halt! It was the King of the Dark Caverns himself who gave that order. 'To me, and to me alone,' he cried, 'belongs the task of destroying these robbers; mine is the hand that shall deal the merited vengeance!'

And as he stalked with gigantic strides up the pathway of dead and dying, he waved over his head the tremendous falchion that hung night and day by the side of the black marble throne in the cavern—a sword, indeed, of potent temper, forged in the bosom of volcanoes, whetted on the threshold of the nether-world.

The air whistled as three times he whirled it round his head, and prepared to strike, when——!

The morning sun rose, and peeped over the hill as if it had been disturbed by the tumult, its bright beams shining straight on the face of the King of the Dark Caverns. His crown gleamed as white flame in the sunshine, and the pearls on his sable robe shone like the seven hunters in the heavens when the night is clear.

Then, with a clap as if a million snuff-boxes were being shut by a million thumbs, the parchment ears of all that vast crowd rang on each forehead to cover the toadstool eyes from the hated beams. Wild was the rush, anywhere, everywhere; some blindly over the precipice, some into the loch, some into the forest, all attempting to regain the gate of the caverns. Panic-struck and without sight they fell over each other, each treading his fellow-fugitive down in his frantic endeavours.

For one instant the king stood up as if turned to stone; then, with a yell of baffled rage, he flung himself backward on the ground and began scooping out the earth like a superhuman mole, seeking an entrance into the bowels of the mountain, if perchance he might find thus a way to his dominions, and the stones and divots flew up behind him as if discharged from a catapult.

'I'll have that gentleman, at any rate,' said the cat, and with one bound he was after the king; but the king in two moments was as many yards into the mountain, and the sable robe of swansdown, into which he had imbedded his claws, was all the cat got, in addition to a fearsome crack on the bridge of his snout from an ascending boulder of granite—the parting salute of the vanished potentate.

'It's an ill wind that blows nobody some good,' said the cat; 'this robe will do to wrap my old dame up in; she must be getting cold by this time.'

So he spread the robe out on the hillside, and took the dame and her shawl and the diamond crown, and rolled them all together like a sausage into it. Then, taking the burden up in his teeth, he cantered leisurely homewards.

Now whom should he see at the door of the dame's cottage but an old pedlar, with a bag of gold in one pocket and a bag of silver in the other, selling copper saucepans to the neighbourhood, a pile of which vessels he carried one on the top of the other above his head.

The cat showed him the crown of a single diamond and the robe of sable feathers, studded with pearls, and the pedlar gave the cat the bag of gold for the diamond crown and the bag of silver for the sable robe; and so pleased was he with his bargain that he gave the cat his wallet full of choice provisions, and a couple of his best saucepans to cook them into the bargain.

'Now,' said the cat, 'take three hairs out of my tail, and tickle the nose of this dame with them, for we must get her out of this faint somehow.'

But the pedlar, after walking round the cat, said he was sorry, but he could not manage to do that anyhow.

'If you don't,' said the cat, 'I will make collops of you.'

'But I can't,' whimpered the pedlar, for he was frightened at the cat's fierce looks.

'Why not?' said the cat.

'Because, because, your honour has not got a tail to pull the hairs out of,' blubbered the pedlar.

'Bless me!' said the cat, 'I had quite forgotten all about that. Never mind, pull three hairs out of my whiskers; that may perhaps do as well.'

The pedlar did so, and the dame, feeling her nose tickled, sneezed as if she had tasted mustard; and getting up, she placed her hands at her side to take hold of her skirts to make a curtsy before asking the pedlar and the cat to enter her house. But finding no skirts to take hold of, and looking down and seeing how scanty was her costume, she fled into the house without another word, and locked herself up in the cupboard; whereupon the cat told the pedlar to go about his business, which he did.

The pedlar gone, the cat entered the cottage, and told the dame to come out of the cupboard.

'I won't,' said the dame, 'as long as that pedlar's present.'

'Don't be silly,' said the cat; 'he's gone, and there's only a cat in the house.'

So the dame came out of the cupboard.

Then the cat poured out all the gold and the silver and the food on to

the floor, and put the saucepan full of water on the hearth to boil. And
the dame, when she saw the gold and the silver and all the choice
provisions, was so delighted that she rocked backwards and forwards
on her chair and smacked herself all over.

As for the cat, he purred so that the embers of the fire were soon in a
bright blaze, and before one could say Scissors the breakfast was
bubbling and hissing in the saucepans.

Then the dame ate and drank, and the cat ate and drank, and
everything was cheerful—the sun looked into the window, the robins
tapped at the sill, singing a song of welcome home, and the hoodie,

looking down the chimney, sniffed the rich food and said, 'My certes, how our old dame is enjoying herself!'

'Now,' said the dame to the cat, 'what am I to do to you in return for all your kindness?'

'Scratch Tom,' said the cat.

'That I will do with pleasure,' said the dame, and she scratched the cat's back with the toasting-fork till he purred again and again, and the sparks flew up the chimney.

And I'm sure it was not much to do for all his trouble, was it?

WALTER DOUGLAS CAMPBELL
Beyond the Border, 1898, illus by Helen Stratton

BITTER-SWEET CAT

She nearly lived in the West End. She'd had to settle for slightly too far south, a street less desired, less at the heart of that tiny world. Its grey tenements stood closer to the dead docklands and the Clyde than to the University and the green slopes of Kelvingrove. It had been built in moneyed times, confidently and respectfully named for some Victorian grandee, and its respectability had attenuated with the fame of its namesake.

The youth strode along on the shadowed side until he came to the number he wanted. He stepped into a close that was dank and smelt of cats. Flight on flight of stairs led upwards, each grey stone step worn smooth and concave in the middle and the dull heavy scuffing of his shoes was the only sound. Just one flight had been recently cleaned, telling of some old wife, perhaps born in this close, who still felt impelled to take a mop over her stairs.

At this time of day the stairhead lights were not lit and all the doorways were darkened. Some had sets of storm doors fully closed against the day; one or two retained the original wood and coloured glass; the rest had solid wooden doors painted in various shades, with spy-holes at eye-level. The viscid aroma from the cheap curry restaurant on the ground floor next door hung in wait for him on every flight.

She lived on the top floor, and as the skylight drew him upward he framed an image of himself as a diver breaking to the bright surface. He stood catching his breath, feeling a little unfit, not bothering to feel guilty about it. His slim form was staring blankly back at him in the door's opaque glass. Above the bell were half a dozen names on slips of card in so many hands and shades of ink. He said hers to himself like a kind of conjuration. He rang the bell purposefully and waited, purpose draining away.

She came to answer the door herself. They looked a moment at each other, then she loosed that nervous smile that always fell coldly on his diffidence and made him doubt his welcome.

'Hi,' she said, 'I thought it would be you.'

He followed her in towards the open door of her room and the music leaking out of it: a taut male voice against bright guitar chords. Cat Stevens today, oh well. He followed, eyes on her long black hair and the pulse of her hips in a long green dress. Her scent hung briefly in the hall's dingy air.

The room was quite warm today, its dowdiness almost effaced by the fine spring sunlight through the half-open window. The flat red and blue of its painted panels shimmered on the faded carpet. 'Sit down while I put the kettle on.'

She shooed her cat from the tattered armchair over which she'd thrown a gaudy shawl. She walked slowly over to the alcove near the window and filled a kettle from a wash-hand basin. She plugged it in and sat it on the floor where she squatted silently, as if fascinated. She turned her head, her screen of hair shifting softly, as the black cat sprang up to the window-sill and crept out to stretch its length on the ledge outside.

He looked around abstractedly. There was the narrow bed, half-buried under a jumble of clothes. The familiar prints and posters: the Picasso, the Van Goghs. The portable record-player on the floor in a scatter of albums. He recognised the covers of Joni Mitchell, Leonard Cohen, the Eagles. On the sofa, where he knew she liked to curl up when reading, lay a random pile of books, magazines and hand-written notes. Two volumes were open, face down: *Titus Groan*, and *The Strange Death of Liberal England*.

'Been working?' he asked as she came to perch on the arm of his chair. Her casual nearness was hard for him to take.

'Yeah, sort of. I'm trying to get the reading done for that horrible essay before I go back home.'

She rose again, lifted her cigarettes from the low coffee-table, lit one and puffed out a cloud of smoke. Then, the kettle boiling, she set the cigarette on the ashtray's edge and went to wash out two mugs.

He watched the smoke curling and writhing, illuminated in the sunny air, spreading and stretching ever thinner into blue-grey haze. His eyes fell on the cat basking in the sunshine and the warm surf of traffic noise. He saw its black frame tense, immediately feral and staring-eyed as a pigeon flew closely by. He was not fond of cats and this particular creature was always ready with the claws for him.

They took coffee and spoke nothings at each other, both aware of why he'd made a point of being here today, this last day before the Easter holidays. She had been hoping he would not turn up too depressed or too earnest. When he had on that great long face it could drag her down from the lighest of moods until she longed to shout at him to cheer up or get off his backside and do something positive. She wasn't ready to accept his eagerness to love forever on their few weeks' acquaintance. She wanted to say 'We're too alike. We can too easily be bad for each other,' but she always held back. So kind had he been, his feelings so trustingly undisguised, that a sort of love (not one he would have coveted) had bound her to him.

Today, he knew and she feared that he was going to say something; something perhaps clumsy, certainly embarrassing; something to establish a commitment. After a week or two of running through the scene in his head he was still shy enough of her reaction to be at a loss for nerve. He felt his stomach twinge. He was drinking his coffee too quickly. Each time he got ready to speak his mind she would be changing the record, making more coffee, fidgeting and talking animatedly about anything. Then, quite suddenly, he put down his mug, looked her full in her half-frowning preoccupied face and simply, determinedly, spoke her name.

'D'you want some wine?' she blurted out. Not looking at him, she got up purposefully from the sofa, fetched a bottle from under the sink and pushed it into his hands. He stared at it as if he'd never seen such a thing. It was Valpolicella, half-empty, with the cork stuffed loosely back in.

'I think it might have gone off,' she said unconcernedly. 'It's been lying since the weekend.'

He tugged out the cork and sniffed the contents. He agreed it smelt a bit funny, but tilted it to his mouth. He swallowed a little and made a face.

'I think you better chuck this out. Unless you want it for cooking, like for sprinkling on your chips.'

He sat the bottle on the table but kept the cork in his hands, which fiddled with it shakily.

'Very witty. Just pour it down the sink, would you?'

His mind buzzing with unspoken words, he made to pick up the bottle, but was stopped short by her sudden cry of fright. She was on her feet, pointing at the window.

'The cat! The cat's fallen off the ledge.'

'What? Are you sure?'

'Yes! She was trying to catch a bird. I saw her falling off. Oh do something!'

They stared a moment at each other, sharing a thought of three floors to the street below, then they both scrambled for the door. He wrenched it open and ran out into the hall, narrowly missing collision with a young woman in a dressing-gown emerging from the bathroom. She threw a loud 'Tut!' after him. He reached the main door first, but was so confused by the various snibs, bolts and latches that he couldn't get it open.

'I'll get it!' she cried, elbowing him aside, and grasped the right handle. As the door was flung open the cat flashed howling past and disappeared into her room. They followed and located the animal under the bed by its mortified yowls.

'Oh God, is she all right? I can't look.'

She sounded ready to cry. He got down on his hands and knees and stuck his head under the bed. He could just make out the black shape against the wall, and he stretched out his hand, making coaxing noises. The cat spat at him and swiftly, effortlessly swiped one set of claws across his hand. He flinched back, banging his head on the under-side of the bed.

'Ah ya ratbag!'

He withdrew his head and was momentarily torn between rubbing his head and putting his injured hand to his mouth.

'Yeah,' he said over his shoulder, 'it's its usual sweet self okay. The wee bugger'll not come out though.'

He slowly got to his feet, thinking what a shock she must have had, deciding now would be a time to take her in his arms. He turned to find her standing with both fists pressed to her mouth, eyes screwed up and two long tear-tracks over her face.

He moved closer and saw that she was shaking with laughter. For a moment he stood frowning, then his own laughter seemed to break like a wave inside him and burst out in great cathartic shouts.

They stood a pace apart: a young woman and a young man laughing with no holding back, more than half at each other, as lovers may never do; free.

MICHAEL MUNRO

GLOSSARY

ase   ashes
anse   heed
ava   at all
bawbee   halfpenny
blate, bleat   bashful
brook   wear
broona   brown one
buk heid   hide-and-seek
burde   board
Burges   Town
campsho   crooked, twisted
cant   playful
carlins   old women
cawin   callin
chafts   cheeks
cluke   claw
coft   bought
crap   crept
creeshie   greasy
daffine   folly
dander   stroll, wander
eith   easy
essi-pattle   a tame grice, or pig, lying about the hearthstone and getting covered with ess, or ashes
foiti   sea name for a mouse
foustie   mouldy
fushionless   feeble
gansell   sauce
gart   made
gommeril   fool
grued   shuddered
gundy   toffee
hint   caught
hurklin   crouching
kebuck   cheese
kiln-ring   open space in front of the fire-place in a kiln
kirn   churn
klooksi   artful trickster
kloora   scratcher

knoost   lump
krami   to scratch
let   stop
limme   let me
lunkin   bobbing up and down
mangerie   feasting
meuting   mewing
mingit   mingled
murti   little thing
mutch   woman's cap
neebin   half awake
nem-kaa'n   name calling
neuks   corners
nignyes   trifies
nyirmi   one who purrs
cust   throw
pale   to test a cheese by incision
pannel   defendant
peesterin   squeaking
perpall   partition
pooshin   poison
preen   pin
redd   tidy
resett   gave shelter to
rottens   rats
scantlie   hardly
scart   scratch
scho   she
scrimply   barely
sets   becomes
skaith   harm
skrovveler   to scrabble
smoored   drowned
soop, soopit   sweep, swept
spang   leap
speir   ask
stra   straw
sych   sighing
tacketty   hobnailed
tenting   seeing
thrum   loose end (of threads)

tine lose
Uponlandis Country
venderin wandering
vengi wanderer
voaleri sea name for cat

waa-cattle sea name for mice
whangs laces
wheen several
winnock window

FURTHER READING

General

Aberconway, Christobel, *A Dictionary of Cat Lovers* (1949)
Briggs, Katharine M, *Nine Lives: Cats in Folklore* (1980)
Currah, Ann, *The Cat Compendium* (1972)
Dale-Green, Patricia, *Cult of the Cat* (1963)
Foster, Dorothy (ed), *In Praise of Cats: An Anthology* (1975)
Gay, Margaret Cooper, *How to Live with a Cat* (1949)
Gooden, Mona (ed), *The Poet's Cat: An Anthology* (1946)
Howey, M Oldfield, *The Cat in the Mysteries of Religion and Magic* [1930]
Kirk, Mildred, *The Everlasting Cat* (1977)
MacBeth, George and Booth, Martin (eds), *The Book of Cats* (1976; pbk 1979)
Necker, Claire, *The Natural History of Cats* (1970)
Ross, Charles Henry, *The Book of Cats* (1868)
Sillar, Frederick and Meyler, Ruth Mary, *Cats Ancient and Modern* (1966)
Stuart, Dorothy Margaret, *A Book of Cats* (1959)

Scottish Cats and Cats by Scottish Authors

Bain, Robert, 'The Cat'; 'The Cat and the Man' (poems in *Mice and Men*, 1941)
Ballantine, RM, *Mee-a-ow! or, good advice to cats and kittens* (1859)
———, *The Robber Kitten* (1858)
———, *Three Little Kittens* (1857)
Bermant, Chaim, *Belshazzar: a cat's story for humans* (1979)
Brown, Bill, 'Cat' (poem in *Lines Review* 64, 1978)
Brown, George Mackay, *Six Lives of Fankle the Cat* (1980; pbk 1984)
Buchan, Peter, 'The Black Cat' (*Ancient Scottish Tales*, 1908)
Campbell, Walter Douglas, 'The Good man of the Inn' (*Beyond the Border*, 1898)
Carrie, Elizabeth, 'The Cat' (poem in *Words* 1, 1976)
Cook, R L, 'Cat' (poem in *Sometimes a Word*, 1963)
Douglas, Sir George, 'Alexander Jones' (*Scottish Fairy and Folk Tales* [1898]; also
    version in Walter Douglas Campbell, *Beyond the Border*, 1898)
Finlay, Campbell K, *Wild Cat Ginger's Family* (1966)
Gordon, Giles, 'The Jealous One' (in *The Illusionist and other fictions*, 1978)
Herriot, James, *Moses the Kitten* (1984)

Jamieson, Robert, 'Lizzie's Lament for her Pet Rabbit which had been killed by the Cat' and 'Cat's Reply' (*see* J Beveridge, *The Poets of Clackmannanshire*, 1885)
——, 'The Lodging House Cat' (The Poet's Box, Mitchell Library)
McHugh, Arthur, 'Cat' (poem in *Lines Review* 81, 1982)
Mackay, R J, *The Little White Cat Among the Heather* (1944)
Macleod, Norman, 'The Spanish Princess' (story of Mull witches as cats in *Reminiscences of a Highland Parish*, 1867)
MacNally, Lea, 'The Scottish Wildcat' (*Scots Magazine*, December 1961)
——, *Highland Year* (1968; pbk 1972)
Maxwell, Gavin, *Ring of Bright Water* (1960; pbk 1972)
Montgomerie, William and Nora (eds), *Scottish Nursery Rhymes* (1964)
Nicoll, Watt and McGinn, Matt, 'The Dundee Cat' (song © Heathside Music, 1969)
Paterson, Aileen, *Maisie Comes to Morningside* (1984)
——, *Maisie Goes to Glasgow* (1984)
——, *Maisie Meets Her Match* (1984) etc.
Poole, Rev George A, *The Exile's Return: or, a cat's journey from Glasgow to Edinburgh* (1837)
Smith, Iain Crichton, 'The Kitten' (poem in *Lines Review* 100, 1987)
Spence, Lewis, 'Mr Mummery and a Mascot' (story in *Scots Magazine*, August 1934)
Stephen, David and Jenkins, David, 'Wildcat' (*Scottish Field*, December 1958)
Stewart, William Grant, 'The Death of John Garve Macgillichallum of Razay' and 'The Gudewife of Laggan' (stories of witches as cats in *The Popular Superstitions and Festive Amusements of the Highlanders of Scotland*, 1823; new edn 1851)
Stuart, Marie W, 'Some Edinburgh Cats' (*Scots Magazine*, January 1946)
Todd, Ruthven, *Space Cat* (1955)
Tomkies, Mike, *My Wilderness Wildcats* (1977; pbk 1978)

INDEX OF AUTHORS, ARTISTS
AND SOURCES

The editor and publisher are grateful to all authors, agents, publishers and other copyright holders who have given permission to print copyright material. Every effort has been made to trace copyright holders, and where this has proved impossible, and the work has been included in the anthology, it is with apologies and in the hope that such use will be welcomed.

All the artists and authors in this anthology are listed below in alphabetical order. Names of copyright holders etc., are added where appropriate, followed by the titles of prose, poem or illustration, the titles (in brackets) of books or journals in which they have already appeared, then by the page number(s) in this book where they are to be found.